**'Ask me what I'm doing in your chair.'**

Emma said coolly, 'This is your ward. If you're here, then you're here for a reason, and I know you won't be slow to tell us all what it is.' She couldn't resist adding tartly, 'And probably loudly.'

The full lips opened sensuously in a tiny smile. 'I came to apologise.' When she said nothing, Simon said, 'Lost for words, Emma? That must be a first for you.'

**Dear Reader**

Although we don't move out of England this month, we do tackle some quite different subjects. In THE STORM AND THE PASSION by Jenny Ashe, Emma has a moral question to face, while Kate in SOMEBODY TO LOVE by Laura MacDonald wonders if she can cope with a short-term affair. In TO DREAM NO MORE by Patricia Robertson, Claire has to overcome fear, while Briony in VET IN POWER by Carol Wood has to overcome the bitterness generated by the feud between her family and Nick's. Problems galore—will our heroines win through?

*The Editor*

Lancashire born, **Jenny Ashe** read English at Birmingham, returned home with a BA and rheumatoid arthritis. Married in Scotland to a Malaysian-born junior surgeon, she returned to Liverpool with three Scottish children when her husband became a GP in 1966. She has written non-stop since then—articles, short stories, radio talks, and novels. She considers the medical environment compassionate, fascinating and completely rewarding.

**Recent titles by the same author:**

THE CALL OF LOVE
TENDER MAGIC

# THE STORM AND THE PASSION

BY

JENNY ASHE

MILLS & BOON LIMITED
ETON HOUSE 18-24 PARADISE ROAD
RICHMOND SURREY TW9 1SR

*First published in Great Britain 1993*
*by Mills & Boon Limited*


*This edition 1993*

ISBN 0 263 78187 9

*Set in 10 on 12 pt Linotron Baskerville*
*03-9308-55559*

*Typeset in Great Britain by Centracet, Cambridge*
*Made and printed in Great Britain*

# CHAPTER ONE

EMMA parked her car and got out to look round. A new life, but not a new place. She had been born not far from here, among the misty Lancashire moors, and now she breathed in deeply, tasting the fresh purity of the unpolluted air, and remembering the view across the grey hospital buildings to the green fields and the gently rolling hills. Early autumn tinted the trees with gold, and a tiny stone inn nestled in a hollow by the side of the road as though it had been there for centuries. The squat tower of the local church stood reassuringly unchanged. Emma breathed out slowly, filled with a peaceful sense of home.

'You'll enjoy working here!' The cheerful nurse who welcomed Sister Emma Sandiford was as bouncy and as jolly as her words. 'We all think Forrestall Hospital is the best in the north of England. In fact——' She stopped and put a plump hand over her mouth, her eyes comically wide.

Emma laughed and put her suitcase on the floor in the hall of the nurses' home while she fumbled for the key she had just been given. 'You can't stop now! In fact what? What dreadful secret are you keeping from me?'

Nurse Briggs winked. 'Take no notice of me, Emma—I'm a terrible chatterer. I was going to say the only fly in the ointment is our chief cardiac surgeon—Simon Warwick. But that isn't being fair to him. He's a good chap really—brilliant, in fact. It's just that he has what some people would call a hasty temper.'

'A crosspatch, eh? Well, that won't bother me. I'm just the opposite—I never get angry.'

'That's good, then, because you're starting on his ward! Now, can I give you a hand to put anything away? Is there anything you want to know about Forrestall?'

Emma smiled again. 'I think you've told me all I need to know for the moment. I come from round here originally, even though I've been an adopted Londoner for eight years. I'll see you later, maybe?'

'I'm off at six. See you in the dining-room, and I'll introduce you to my crowd.'

Simon Warwick. . . Emma had heard of him. He was reputed to be the best outside London, and one of her cardiac textbooks was written by a Mr S.T. Warwick. String of letters after his name. Must be the same man. Well, his textbook was good. She couldn't see how a spot of bad temper now and again would make any difference to her new bright future as sister at Forrestall. And she had to make the move just now—losing Dad so suddenly had left Mum feeling very lonely, and Emma had been working much too far away to be any help. At least now she was only a few miles from home, and could pop over to Gorston whenever she was needed.

Emma surveyed her hospital flat—they were all very much alike, wherever they were. Clean, sparsely furnished. A few bare nails in the wall where the last occupant had removed pictures. Briskly she put away her clothes, and hung up her coat. Neat in a dark skirt and pale blue cotton sweater, she looked out of the window at the northern autumn landscape, the far-off tidy little suburban houses set at the edge of the little northern town, its cotton-mill chimneys no longer the busy hives of activity they used to be, standing idle in the hollow between the moors. For a single moment she felt regret. It had been so much fun in London, and she had made so many friends. But the move had to be made—and a sister on top grade was the best move possible. She nodded at the far rolling fields, where a few small grey sheep grazed like painted scenery, with wispy clouds in a wispy sky. 'I'll soon get to know you again,' she told them. 'It's the job that matters—not the place—and certainly not a hot-tempered chief. Simon Warwick will be the least of my problems!'

'Hey, you, young woman!' A man's voice, cultured but obviously angry about something. Emma had been wandering along beside the hospital tennis courts, finding her way around until it was time to meet Sally Briggs in the dining-room. Across the breadth of a court, someone was gesticulating towards her. She could see even at this distance that he was a handsome figure of a man, tall, youngish, muscular, and lithe, as his body was shown off to advantage by the energetic waving of both arms towards her. But 'Hey, you' and 'young woman'? It wasn't a very polite way of addressing her.

Emma paused in her walk. She had told Sally that she never lost her temper, and that was almost true. But it was also true that she did not approve of bad-mannered people. To be gestured at and shouted at as though she were some naughty servant-girl didn't make Emma very keen to prolong this one-sided conversation. However, he clearly wished to tell her something, and she recommenced her walk, turning in the direction of her handsome, raven-haired inquisitor. Perhaps he was in charge of the tennis courts, and she had inadvertently walked on a white line. She could thing of nothing else she had done since arriving at Forrestall that could possibly cause anyone offence. She could see his eyes now — they were a perfect clear blue, and very attractive indeed. But his voice had irritated her, and she intended to make that clear to him. 'I wonder if you were addressing me, young man?' She used the words deliberately. Her tone was extremely polite and gentle as she reached him, and looked up into those eyes, almost hidden as they were by the shadow of frowning black eyebrows. 'And if so, I wonder why it was necessary to shout? I could hear you very well from the other side of the tennis court, you know.'

His voice was quieter now, but still very uptight about something. 'You must be new. Well, I'm Simon Warwick, and you have taken my——'

Emma swallowed her astonishment just in time, and gathered up the remnants of her courage. 'The cardiac surgeon? But you're so young. . . I believe I've read your textbook.' She realised that she was waffling, and took hold of herself. She said more slowly, 'I'm Emma Sandiford, and I understand I'm your new ward sister.'

'You!'

She saw surprise and curiosity in the blue eyes, but the eyebrows were still down, still furious. To forestall any further outburst, Emma said hastily and rather cheekily, now that she knew who he was, 'I accept your apology.'

'I was not apologising. I was expressing surprise and also disappointment at your——'

'So was I.'

As Mr Warwick quietened down, taken aback by the

coolness of his antagonist, she realised she should never have taken him for a tennis court man—not someone dressed in an expensively tailored grey suit, with shining black shoes and a crimson silk tie. He looked into her eyes with those devastating blue ones, and instead of hectoring anger she now recognised something like resignation. He said, his attractive voice cold now, 'Is that your car parked by the gate?'

'The little Peugeot? Yes, it is.'

'I'd be glad if you'd move it at once.'

'For any particular reason?'

'That space is reserved for me—or for anyone who is deputising for me. It's important that it's kept clear in case of emergencies.'

Emma hadn't taken her eyes from his, and now she said in the same reasonable tones that she had been using during the entire conversation, 'Then of course I'll move it. But there was nothing to indicate that it was reserved. And no need to shout. . . I'll go and get my keys from my flat.'

Simon Warwick turned his eyes up to heaven, before reaching out a hand and taking her arm just above the elbow. With exaggerated politeness this time he said, 'May I?' and he steered her towards the car park. Her little car was neatly parked between two white lines. He pointed towards the rhododendron bushes just in front of the car bonnet. A small notice was fixed on a short post. It read, 'Reserved for Mr Warwick'. He said, heavily sarcastic, 'Nothing to indicate what, Sister Sandiford?'

She removed his hand from her arm, looking down to see the red marks his fingers had made in her skin. 'I saw nothing as I parked. Maybe if you look at it from the driver's seat you'll see that the notice is hidden by a rhododendron branch.'

'God protect me from know-all sisters!' He turned away. 'You realise that I need this space kept free? We often get emergencies, and I'm the only surgeon specialising in this subject. Get your crate out of here—please, Sister?—and I'll forget about it this time. You're lucky I wasn't in a hurry!' And he looked very directly into her eyes for a moment. Something made Emma forget his anger, even his rudeness, as she saw something raw and lonely in the lean face, lines of tension round the sculpted lips and the deep sky-blue eyes. She wasn't annoyed with him any more. And for that moment something inside her responded to an unspoken intimacy. Then the spell broke as he looked away and strode off to his car, which was a long green Jaguar, its driver's door wide open where he had left it to shout to Emma. The tape inside was playing a Mozart quintet. He swung himself into the driving seat and waited, tapping his fingers impatiently on the wheel.

Realising this wasn't the time to prolong an already uncomfortable dialogue, Emma turned and walked quickly—but did not run—back to the nurses' flats. When she returned with her car keys, this incredibly young-looking Simon Warwick was still sitting where she had left him, his fingers still tapping the steering wheel, the Mozart still filling the limousine with beauty that didn't go with the black mood of the driver. Refusing to allow herself to be flurried, she calmly backed her car out, and drove to another space. She heard the roar of the Jaguar engine being revved unnecessarily loudly as he shifted into the vacated space, switched off, got out and slammed the door, before striding like a whirlwind towards the entrance to the cardiac clinic.

Sally Briggs was looking out for her when she went to the dining-room some time later. 'Been doing some sightseeing, Emma?'

'Quite a lot, actually.'

'Why? What did you see?'

'Simon Warwick.'

'You met him? I hope he was nice to you.'

'Oh, yes and no.' Emma smiled at Sally's open-eyed surprise. 'But I have a feeling that my reputation for being calm and reasonable is going to be severely tried and tested in the next few weeks.' And she explained about the ill-natured introduction the new ward sister had had to her chief surgeon. 'I don't know why he had to be so impatient, Sally. There was something—hungry about him. Sad, somehow. Do you think he's had no opposition so far? You mean to tell me that no one has stood up to him?'

'They've tried, honestly they've tried. He can be as sweet as ice-cream when he wants to be. But most of the time he's in a hurry, and impatient with the rest of us common humanity because we aren't as clever and intelligent as he is. Not in his stratosphere.' Sally grinned and said, 'Forget him anyway. Come and meet the girls. You'll find that our little crowd makes up for the bad welcome Warwick's given you.'

Emma was soon laughing with the other nurses, enjoying their broad northern hospitality she remembered from her childhood. 'No,' she answered someone's question, 'I've not left any grieving boyfriends behind me. Yes, I did have a couple of nice chaps, but you know how it is with medical people—they always seem to have to move on, and you lose touch. I'm not complaining. I think I'm going to like it here.' In spite of Mr Warwick's unaccountable moods. She didn't say that aloud.

Sally Briggs said stoutly, 'Of course you are. Even though the first day wasn't up to scratch.'

'It isn't over yet! Why don't I take you all out to that little inn I noticed—the one that's only half a mile up the Manchester Road?'

The girls were appreciative. 'You're going to fit in here very well, Emma! But we'll treat you tonight. You can treat us the day you get your first Forrestall paycheque!' And they walked along the pavement together in the warmth of a late summer evening, the leaves just beginning to turn brown, golden or red, and the odd one or two floating gently down from the trees. The little inn was called the Pendle, and there was a sign with a black-hatted witch flying through the air on a broomstick, a broad smile on her face. With all the gossip and chatter, Emma almost didn't see the long green Jaguar parked in a corner of the Pendle car park.

She said nothing to the others, but inside the low, oak-beamed snug she looked carefully about her. She had been right. In a corner, hidden by a bushy weeping fig plant, she recognised the expensive sleeve of the grey-suited man who had grabbed her arm so tightly that afternoon that the marks had not faded for quite a time. He was alone. And later, when she managed to catch a glimpse of his face, she was appalled by the sadness in it. The blue eyes that she had last seen sparking with anger were downcast, and the slim fingers that had gesticulated at her clung round an untouched glass of bitter. It disturbed her. There was a lot more to Simon Warwick than a clever man with a bad temper. It was none of her business. Yet the more she laughed and chatted with the girls, the more she felt an empathy with the silent, almost tragic figure in the corner, the figure who did not move, and was still there when the girls left the Pendle and made their way back to the hospital, the stars beginning to shine in the blue velvet sky.

Emma was too busy getting to know the patients and other staff in Orchard Ward to brood too much on what she had seen in the inn. The other sister was Welsh, a middle-aged lady called Abina Brown with a family of six to keep her busy. 'I come to work to relax, Emma,' she laughed.

Emma didn't mention Simon Warwick. It was Abina who brought up the subject, on Emma's first full day at work. 'He's operating all morning, and it's a pretty tense time—you know the sort of post-op problems we have. He's a perfectionist, so don't be surprised if we don't all get it right the first time. He's a good sort, Emma—he'll grow on you.'

He already has, thought Emma silently, in some strange way. But she kept her thoughts to herself, and waited as calmly as she could for the first cases to be brought in from Recovery. The bags of saline and cross-matched blood were ready if needed, the drips already set up beside each bed, and the senior houseman went round with Emma checking the case-notes and making sure the correct names were over each clean white bed. Then she checked the oxygen cylinders to make sure they were working. Mr Warwick wasn't going to find the staff under Emma's command lacking in the knowledge of the proper post-op procedures. The three acute beds were closest to her office, and their patients were to be connected to the monitors when they were brought down from Recovery.

The first patient was a young man who had undergone a bypass operation the previous week, had relapsed into unconsciousness afterwards, and only now was beginning to pick up again and show signs of a successful operation. Emma introduced herself and made sure he was comfortable . He didn't need a monitor, but she checked his heart-rate, his temperature and his blood-pressure, as well as the wound in the chest and the long row of stitches in the thigh where the graft had been taken. Emma pronounced herself satisfied with his progress. 'I'm glad, Sister,' he told her. 'I'd hate to disappoint Mr Warwick—he spent so much time patching me up. And that decent Scots bloke in recovery, Charge Nurse MacFarlane—I think I gave him a rough time.'

'You're young to have to go through all this,' Emma remarked.

'Good as new now, honest, Sister.'

'Well, just make sure you don't suffer in silence. If there's anything you need, just press that buzzer, OK?'

Two more cases were sent down, having had a 'balloon' procedure, where their arteries round the heart had been artificially widened. Emma and the houseman, Jerry Green, made them comfortable, while they waited for the final case. 'An abnormality of the ventricle. Had it for years,' Jerry explained, 'but he was so ill that the risks of failure were very high. Only when he was literally on his last legs did Mr Warwick advise that there was no alternative to surgery. I'll just phone Recovery and see how he is.'

But the whispers were already reaching them that the patient was on his way, and that Mr Warwick was with him. Jerry and Emma went to the door to meet them. The white bed was being pushed along the quiet corridor by two porters, with a theatre nurse holding up the drip, and Simon Warwick in his operating greens, mask pulled down beneath his jutting chin, checking the pulse as they walked. Another nurse trotted behind with the patient's notes and an expression of apprehension.

Mr Warwick's eyes didn't leave his patient's face until he was settled and his eyes had opened after the anaesthetic. Then the consultant looked up, and straight into Emma's eyes. She felt the thrill of recognition of his good looks, especially those eyes the very colour of midsummer. 'Sister.' It was a brief acknowledgement. 'This is Joe Broadhurst. You know the history?'

'Yes, Jerry—er—Dr Green was explaining it to me.'

'Mac wants you to look after him. He needs the bed in Recovery. You know what to do—it's quite straightforward. Bleep me at once if you're worried.'

'Of course, Doctor.'

He straightened up, and for a moment seemed strangely reluctant to look away from his petite new sister's heart-shaped face and big brown eyes. She felt a surge of electricity between them, and imagined that he felt it too. Then he recalled himself, and turned to Jerry. 'Have you done a ward round this morning, Green?'

'Yes, sir. If you have a moment, I'd like to have a word about the mitral valve replacement. The patient is very restless. I don't think it can be infection—she's still on a high dosage of antibiotics.'

'Just nerves, maybe. It upsets them when they first realise they can hear the sound of the clicking. But come along, let's take a look. Sister?'

'I have the notes here, Mr Warwick. It's Mary Morris, isn't it?'

Another glance in Emma's direction—surely it couldn't be grudging approval?—before he swung on his heel and strode along the ward, followed by Jerry Green and Emma. Again she thought how athletic and young he looked—only a year or so older than the twenty-one-year-old Jerry, yet he had to be over thirty, surely. He had been a specialist for years—Emma had still been a student when she had read his book. He must be very active—maybe a fitness enthusiast. Whatever gave him that figure, noticeable even under the shapeless hospital greens, it was a pleasure to watch him move. Emma blushed as they reached the bed of the valve patient, and Simon Warwick turned suddenly towards Emma and held out his hand for the operation notes. She comforted herself with the thought that he was too busy to have noticed her blush, still less to realise that it was his physical attributes that had caused it.

'Thank you, Sister.' The voice could be quite gentle at times, musical, deep and caressing, reminding her of that Mozart quintet that he had been playing on his car stereo. Jerry turned too, as though he recognised that his chief was being suddenly uncharacteristically polite; but he looked away at once, as though it was none of his business. Emma remained beside them both, as Simon Warwick examined the fluttery little woman with the newly replaced mitral valve in her heart, and reassured her that she was doing very nicely. She looked up at her surgeon with adoring thanks. Emma automatically picked up the notes when Mr Warwick had finished, and followed the two doctors back to the office.

'Clinic in a couple of minutes.' Simon Warwick looked at his watch—expensive, probably a Rolex. 'Still, I don't think they'll mind waiting while we have a cup of tea, Sister?'

'Of course.' Emma had noticed the kettle on the window-ledge, and she hastily plugged it in, seeing Jerry again registering surprise, as though Mr Warwick seldom paused in his workload for a simple cup of tea. 'Do you both take sugar?'

Simon Warwick looked up from his paperwork and actually smiled, the blue eyes crinkling at the corners, his face lighting up, transformed. 'No indeed. Caffeine is bad enough without adding yet another cardio-pathogen, Sister.' And as she handed the beaker back. 'Don't forget, Sister—I want to be informed about Mr Broadhurst.'

'Yes, Sir.'

And again he paused very briefly and looked back at her from under those forbidding black brows, before striding off with a rustle of his operation clothes, his muscular arms reaching up behind his neck to untie the mask as he vanished. Emma suppressed an intake of breath at the effect this dynamic young surgeon had on her. From anger and a cold resentment at their first meeting in the car park, Simon Warwick was showing a much more definite interest in her. And it was an interest she shared, after that intriguing glimpse of him deep in solemn contemplation in the inn the previous night, when he thought no one was looking at him. There was a lot more to Simon Warwick than a clever mind and skilful hands. . .

She turned to see Jerry Green grinning. 'What's so funny?' she asked.

'I've never seen the chief look twice at any nurse. Must be those big brown eyes, Emma. He's not the sociable type. You must have made something of an impression.'

'I did yesterday.' To hide her embarrassment, she told Jerry about parking in the reserved spot. 'He was very cross.'

'But it certainly made him notice you,' smiled Jerry, draining his cup and putting it down. 'I'd say——'

Emma interrupted quite tersely. 'Don't bother saying anything. He was rude to me—and today he wasn't so rude. That's all there is to it, Jerry. Anyway, he must surely have a wife and family, so you shouldn't say things like that.'

'True. I know there is a Mrs Warwick—also in hospital work, I believe. But no one seems to have met her.'

Emma wanted to ask more, but was too sensible to let anyone know about her interest. Instead she said, 'I'll just go and see Joe Broadhurst, and Mary Morris. The chief did say to keep a close eye on them.'

'OK. I'll be in my room catching up on some sleep.'

Emma was glad to be left alone. She walked slowly round the ward, familiarising herself with the names and diseases of the patients, and stopping to chat to some of them about their personal problems. 'We'll follow you up after you leave here. Don't worry. We've got a Lifestyle leaflet, and a phone number for you to ring if you're not sure about anything. When you come back to outpatients, you'll see a physician who specialises in your kind of problems, but Mr Warwick is always here if you need him. Let's hope you don't, eh? One operation is quite enough for anyone!'

Back in the corridor, she was just going into her room when she heard a stifled noise in the sluice, and, opening the door, she found a student nurse in floods of tears. 'What on earth's the matter, love? Aren't you well?'

'Mr Warwick,' sniffed the girl. 'He shouted at me. Told me I was lazy and letting down the other people in the ward.'

'And were you?' asked Emma gently.

'I—yes, I had stopped for a rest. I've got my period and I had terrible stomach cramps. It's—it's better now. It was just—the way he told me off—as though I were a naughty kid.'

Emma didn't reply at once. She couldn't judge without hearing the full story. But she knew she needed every member of staff on duty in Orchard Ward, not weeping in the loo. There were just too many patients who required supervision. 'Don't let him get to you, Rachel. Just get back to work. If you feel bad again, come and tell me and I'll find you an analgesic. Better still, report in early, in time to find a replacement if you aren't up to the work.'

'Thanks, Sister. I didn't mean to malinger, honest. If only he'd spoken gently, as you did.'

Yes, Mr Simon Warwick did appear to have problems in speaking gently to anyone apart from his patients. Yet that morning there had been something about the look she had received from those blue eyes, and the musical voice he had used when speaking to Emma. . . She took a deep breath. These were early days. But when she knew her irascible chief a little better she meant to take him to task for reducing her nurses to quivering tearful masses. It was uneconomic use of the workforce, and he had to be told.

The rattle of trolleys and the unmistakable smell of mashed potatoes reminded Emma of the time. She hurried along to the office to check if any of the patients were on special diets before the lunches were served. The notice was on the wall, and she was beginning to scan the list when a deep voice said, 'It's all right, Emma, Sister Brown has already checked.'

Simon Warwick was sitting in her chair, at her desk, his long legs in smart grey flannels stretched out as though he was quite at home. He wore a starched white coat now, and his long slim fingers were playing casually with a gold pen. His dark hair was neatly combed back, waving slightly from his intelligent square forehead. 'Go on, ask me what I'm doing in your chair.'

She didn't rise to the bait. Instead she said coolly, 'This is your ward. If you're here, then you're here for a reason, and I know you won't be slow to tell us all what it is.' She couldn't resist adding tartly, 'And probably loudly.'

If she expected an outburst, none came. Instead the full lips opened sensuously in a tiny smile, showing even white teeth, and the eyes crinkled at the corners. 'It isn't hospital business, Emma.'

'In that case I'll just go and see to the lunches.'

'No—wait.'

'Why?'

'I came to apologise.'

Jerked out of her routine by the unexpected remark, she swung round to face him. His smile broadened. When she said nothing, he said, 'Lost for words, Emma? That must be a first for you.'

'Apologising must be a first for you.' She looked down, her breathing becoming a little irregular. What was this man playing at? Whatever it was, it disturbed her. And those legs, the muscles apparent under the expensive cloth, the white coat casually open. . . 'I really must go.'

'No.' The word shot out like a bullet.

'Then tell me what you want.'

'I want to say I'm very sorry for speaking to you as I did yesterday. I've seen the way you work this morning, and I've come to the conclusion that I was hasty. You're a damn good nurse, and such as you are hard to find.'

'Oh, is that all?'

'You're not impressed? Simon Warwick never says sorry.'

'That's nothing to be proud of. I have a young nurse reduced to tears this morning. You wouldn't care to say sorry to her? She was out of commission for a good half-hour when she ought to have been working.' Emma was pleased with her own restraint. She had told Simon Warwick exactly what she thought, but without raising her voice.

His voice lost the gentleness then. 'That child was reading one of those ridiculous love-comics—you know the ones that are all pictures, with balloons coming out of their mouths? I wouldn't tolerate that on duty, and I expect you to agree with me on that.' He rose to his feet. 'I take it my visit here was useless? You intend to go on being piqued because I didn't fall like everyone else at your beautiful feet at first sight?'

She looked up, amazed. 'But—it isn't like that at all.' He thought her beautiful? Did that explain his extra-keen glances of that morning? 'Mr Warwick, you're entitled to your hasty temper. It doesn't bother me, so long as the ward runs smoothly. Is that plain enough for you?'

Simon Warwick nodded. 'Quite.' She watched him open the door and leave without a backward look. Emma reached for the back of the chair and sank into her own seat, feeling a certain weakness of the knees. As she brushed her forehead with the back of her hand, she noticed that her fingers were shaking. She had been right; working here was certainly going to test all her resources.

Weakly she looked up at the wall-sheet. 'I need a holiday! When is my next weekend off?' And she was only half joking.

# CHAPTER TWO

'So YOU really don't mind coming back to work in the north, love?' Emma's mother was a quiet lady, with simple tastes. Her world had revolved around her husband, and she was quite lost without him to fuss over. Mr Sandiford had been a lecturer at the local technical college, and led an uneventful life—which made his sudden death from a heart attack a cruel surprise to all the family.

'No, I don't mind, Mum. The pay is better, even though I lose my London weighting. Money goes further. And I've made a few friends in the hospital.'

Her mother was sitting uncomfortably on the edge of the chair, holding her cup and saucer at an angle. Emma gently took it from her and said, 'You've been jumpy ever since I came this afternoon. What is it? Were you going to go out? Don't mind me. I'm just glad to have my old room as it was, and relax. Don't let me interfere with your plans.'

'Well—no, I'm not going out. Your aunty Beryl might pop in later to make sure I'm all right. But——'

'Go on, Mum! What's on your mind? I can see you're on pins.'

Her mother hesitated, then blurted out, 'It's Christmas plans, love. Beryl wants me to go on a cruise with her. I've never ever spent Christmas away from Gorston—and now that you'll be here it seems all wrong. But the doctor told me I ought to keep busy, and it was nice of Beryl to get the brochures, and——'

'Oh, shut up, Mother!' laughed Emma. 'I think it's a great idea. I insist on it. Anyway,' she lied, 'I'm working over the Christmas week, so you two would be here on your own. I'm so glad you've got it sorted out. Now we're both happy.'

She was off duty for the weekend. But though she tried to relax, her thoughts were still busy with her first few weeks at Forrestall, and with the disturbing and attractive Simon Warwick. What did make him tick? And why did he seem so isolated from the rest of the hospital staff, drinking all alone, and looking so thoughtful and moody?

When Beryl, her father's sister, came for her usual visit in the evening, Emma made an excuse that she needed to get some things from the corner shop, and after the usual pleasantries with her relatives she slipped out to the car and drove along the main road towards the Pendle Inn. She didn't mean to stop. But somehow her subconscious had already slowed the car, thrust the gear into second, indicated, and turned into the inn car park. She sat there for some minutes, her heart beating noticeably. Now why had her subconscious behaved so unpredictably?

She looked surreptitiously around at the other cars. No Jaguar. What did she expect? It was Saturday night, and all sensible consultants were at home with their wives, unless they were out to dinner. The light was fading. It would soon be winter. The wind was shaking the branches of the trees and the hedgerows, and the sky was angry. She tried to reason with herself—It's ten years since you were fifteen and did this sort of thing over lads! She was annoyed with herself, yet she knew she couldn't settle at home. Simon Warwick disturbed her, and his powerful image, both arrogant yet mysteriously appealing, was constanly haunting her. She took a deep breath. She had better go home. Yet her limbs refused to obey her, and she sat immobile in the car, listening to the wind, and the occasional bursts of laughter from the pub drifting across the car park.

Suddenly she heard footsteps scrunching on the gravel, and felt a touch of fear. Lone females didn't sit in cars in looming night. The footsteps stopped very close to her, and she was conscious of the remaining light being blocked out by a human figure. She locked her fingers together so that the nails bit into her skin. Then someone's knuckles tapped lightly on the window. Swallowing her fear, she looked up. It was Simon Warwick, dressed in jeans and a sweater covered by a fawn anorak, his black hair wild against the wild sky. And somehow she wasn't surprised to see him. She unlocked her fingers, wound the window down, and tried to make her voice casual. 'Oh, hello.'

His voice was deep, and some of the words were lost in the gusts. But she knew what he was saying. 'How long have you been here?'

'I'm not sure. I just—thought I'd pop in and see if any of the girls were here.'

'They're not. Who'd go out on a night like this?' As he spoke spatters of rain began to cover the car windows, and he smoothed the hair from his eyes. 'Like a drink? Seeing that you've come all this way?'

'It isn't far. There wasn't much going on at home. . .' She locked the car door and followed him into the shelter of the inn porch. They both paused to tidy their hair and wipe the rain from their faces. Her heart was racing with the excitement of the encounter.

'Why did you really come?' His look was very direct, and his voice was full of sincerity.

Emma felt a sexual force inside her responding to those potent eyes, a force that shocked her by its intensity. She tried hard to be casual. 'Does it matter? I do have a private life, you know.'

'Yes, damn it, it matters!' His temper sparked. But he took a breath, controlled himself and pushed open the door. 'Let's go in. I can't shout at anyone inside in case I get arrested!' It was an attempt at humour, but his eyes weren't smiling.

She walked to the corner where she had first seen him. They took off their coats before he said, 'Why did you sit here?' He turned away for a moment to hang the coats on a stand. 'And don't try to put me off this time. I'd like an answer that makes sense.'

She was watching the grace of his body as it twisted back from the coat-stand, and he sank into the chair beside her. Their faces were very close, and his eyes so intense that she knew she could hide nothing from him. He would see through any white lies she might try. She said quietly, 'I saw you here one night.'

'Why didn't you come and speak to me?'

'I was with the girls.'

'Otherwise you would have come?'

She hesitated. The blue gaze was unwavering. 'Yes, I think I would. You——'

'Go on, Emma.'

'You looked very—alone. But then again, you might have been glad of the peace, after a long day operating. . .' But if he wanted peace, why was he not at home with his family? 'Your wife was working, maybe.'

'Is that what you thought?'

'Vaguely, I suppose. I wasn't really consciously thinking about why you were there. . .' But her voice trailed away as his sky-blue lie detectors flickered. She said quickly, 'Well, are we having that drink?'

'Sorry.' He turned towards the bar without asking her what she wanted, and came back with a bottle of chilled white wine and two glasses. 'Don't look so worried—I don't expect you to drink it all. I'm allowed to—I'm not in the car.' He poured two glasses and handed one to her. 'Well, here's to—something or other.' His voice was suddenly weary, and she was reminded of the way he had sat so still, his fingers gripping the untouched bitter the last time she had been in the Pendle. He swirled the wine, and sipped it. Emma did the same.

For a while they didn't speak. Around them the snug was crowded with regulars. Someone was playing darts, and there was a buzz of conversation, and a crackle of a real log fire. Emma said, 'It's very relaxing, just listening.'

Simon nodded. 'That's why I come. I watch life, Emma—I don't take part in it.'

She put her glass down. 'The strong silent type? Don't you think you ought to explain that? You play a very vital part in a great many people's lives. How can you say you only watch it?'

For the first time that lift of the generous mouth signalled a slight smile, and she warmed to him for making the effort. 'Well,' he said, his voice marginally more cheerful, but skilfully fielding her questions, 'that's enough about me for one night. Tell me your story, Emma. Tell me why such a pretty girl spends a Saturday night alone, for one thing. Have you any boyfriends still in London? You're pining!'

'No, I'm not,' she retorted. She was very conscious of

the brusque yet charming way he had turned the conversation away from himself. 'And I'm not pretty either—I know that.'

'Don't argue with someone older and wiser, Sandy.' Sandy! It was a nickname she had had at school. After school, only one man had ever used it, and he had gone off with her best friend. . . Again Simon was quick to notice her reaction. 'You don't like being called that?'

'I—I like it very much actually. It's just that—hardly anyone has used it since my schooldays.'

'That's nice. Then when I'm in a bad temper in the ward I'll use it, and you'll know that I'm not angry with you. Not with you—only with life in general.'

'Why? Can you tell me? Why do you lose your temper so much?'

He drained his glass, and poured more wine. Then he smiled a proper smile, and she felt that weakness in her body, that reaction to him she had no control over, and was glad she was sitting down. He never smiled at anyone else. He never apologised. Yet he had done both for her. He said with open good humour, 'Because I'm a consultant, my dear Sandy. Don't you know that consultants can do what they like?'

'You don't mean that, Mr Warwick.'

'My name is Simon, and I want you to use it, Sandy.' He paused and said honestly, 'No, I know it would make for more harmonious working conditions if I could control my impatience at times. But they know me at Forrestall. They take me as they find me, and I like that.'

There was another companionable silence. Although it was peaceful in their little corner, Emma felt the blood rushing in her ears, knew that adrenalin was flowing all the time she was with this handsome stranger. Because he was still a stranger, a man with a secret. And she knew she didn't want the night to end. Being with him was something she wanted. Just being there, nothing more. And listening to that wonderful voice, the voice that reminded her that Simon Warwick knew so much more about life than Sandy Sandiford. The wine had loosened his tongue a little, but he was still giving nothing away. Emma wondered if she dared ask more questions. She said, 'I thought your textbook for nurses was very good, you know.'

'Thank you. That was a while ago.'

'Yes. But I remember wondering why such an expert as you wasn't working in a London hospital—maybe Harley Street, instead of an out-of-the-way place like Forrestall.'

He said nothing for a moment, his look directed into the glowing flames of the fire. Then, again steering the question away, as though fielding a ball, he said, 'I could ask you the same question. You left London, didn't you?'

'Yes—but for family reasons. . .' And again she left her sentence unfinished, as she realised Simon Warwick's reason must be the same. His wife. Did she forbid him to move, or did she enjoy working here? Emma dared not ask again. She didn't want to lose the feeling of closeness that had developed almost imperceptibly between them.

He poured her a second glass, but she made him take half away. He refilled his own glass from hers, and the familiarity of the gesture filled her with a strange joy. She pictured what they looked like to the other customers—the tall and very good-looking man chatting up one of the nurses. 'Do I look like a nurse?' she asked.

He smiled again. 'You don't know? My dear, you

look like a beautiful elf, with your lovely eyes filled with the wisdom of the ages, and your berry-brown hair curled untidily round your very wise face—as though you'd just got out of your bed under a toadstool.'

She was disconcerted by the impact of his suddenly beautiful words. No one had ever said anything quite so touching to her. 'How old do I look?' she asked.

'Either ten or a hundred. I'm not sure which.' Was it the wine talking, or Simon Warwick? He went on, 'All I know is that when I set out to walk to the pub tonight two magpies flew across the road into the fields, and I remember thinking, Two for joy. Wouldn't it be nice if I met Sandy tonight?'

'You—you thought that?'

Something in her voice alerted him. 'Why? Did you think that too?'

'I came, didn't I?'

'You didn't mean to come?'

'I don't think so, Simon. The car seemed to—find its own way.' She felt a little scared suddenly. She didn't believe in witches. But there might be some power that Simon Warwick could exert over her. . . She decided to say nothing at all about it ever again.

But he was staring at her now, and she knew he was thinking the same thing. Some sort of telepathy, maybe. Emma hated leaving him, especially now, but the feeling of apprehension wouldn't go away, and suddenly she stood up and said, 'I ought to get back. I didn't tell Mum where I'd be. She didn't worry about me in London, but out here, knowing I'm alone in the dark and the rain, she might worry.'

'I understand, Sandy.' He looked up into her eyes, and she longed to put her arms round him and hug him to her, press her cheek against his and take away the loneliness. But he rose then, and helped her with her coat before taking his own. They said nothing as they walked out to the cool of the blustery night. As Emma walked towards her car Simon put out his hand to steady her against the wind, and she allowed herself to lean against him a little, pretending the wind was stronger than it really was. She felt protected. Yet as the wind blew the creaking inn sign she looked up into the cheerful face of the Pendle witch, and felt, too, a tiny tremor of fear.

The rain had started again, and her hair was very wet. She looked like an elf, Simon had said. And wise eyes. . . She stopped as they reached the car, and she looked up with a forced smile. 'Thank you for the drink.'

He said nothing, but drew her roughly against him, holding her tightly with both arms so that she couldn't move her own. When he bent and kissed her lips, the rain pelted even more, so that their kiss was wet with raindrops that he gently licked with his tongue from her lips. She tried to disguise the shiver of her eager response, but as soon as he loosened his grip her own arms went round him, and she leaned her cheek against the damp cloth of his anorak. They stood, two people as one, for a long time. How many minutes? Ten or a hundred?

Emma fumbled a little with the car lock. When she had settled herself in the driving seat and fastened her seatbelt, she looked up at Simon. Neither of them spoke. He was outlined, a dark shape against a wild ragged sky, his face lit pallidly by the single lamp that burned in the car park. Emma twisted the key, and the engine burst into life. She took off the handbrake, and didn't look back as she drove out on to the main road, windscreen wipers at high speed in the face of the driving rain, and turned the car towards her home.

She lay awake for a long time that night, staring up at the white ceiling, listening to the downpour outside, and sensing the turmoil inside her own heart. Something had happened that night, but she didn't know what it was. Only time would reveal the reality of the magic of the Pendle witch. Was it good or bad? Whatever it was, she still felt the power inside her, the invisible thread that linked her so powerfully to Simon—to another woman's husband. That was bad. It had to be fought, and fight it she would. When she met Simon on Monday, she vowed she would make no reference to their chance meeting. . .yet it hadn't been chance at all. . .

Back at work, Monday morning had turned into a beautiful autumn day, full of golds and red and rich browns. Emma greeted the patients, pleased to find herself popular and welcome now that they knew her. She was no longer 'the new sister' but their own Sister Sandiford, and they knew they could call her and she would listen with patience to their little problems as well as their big ones. She admired the flowers by the beds, noting how a blue sky always made everything look better. The sky, through the windows, was almost cloudless today, and for a moment Emma stood staring at it, wondering why she felt so moved by it. Then she heard a scuffle of hurrying nurses, and a loud voice in the corridor, and realised why the sky was familiar—it was the same colour as Simon Warwick's eyes.

Rachel, her little junior, was scarlet with her efforts to get to the ward before Mr Warwick. Puffing, she scurried down the centre of the ward to the ward station, where she did her best to disappear behind the desk. Unfortunately she sent flying a pile of pre-operation forms, and had to pick every one up under the lowering gaze of their chief consultant. Emma quickly went forward to help her, but Simon said, 'Leave those, Sister—I need you here.'

It could almost be a different man altogether from the lonely person she had met in the car park of the inn—the man who had described her as an elf who looked as though she slept under a toadstool. . . Emma almost laughed aloud at the contrast, as Simon, with Jerry Green in tow, laid down his list of tomorrow's operations and demanded to know if they were all fit for anaesthetic. 'It's no use wasting my time seeing them this morning if they're not.'

Quietly she took the list and scanned it. 'This lady's blood-pressure hasn't come down with diuretics, sir. Do you want the anaesthetist to see her again? And Mrs Calby has a chest infection.'

'On top of her LV failure? I'll take a look.' He waited for Emma to lead him to the patients in question, while she drew the curtains around them, and made sure their notes were ready at his elbow. She watched him at work, unable to stop herself admiring the sheer male beauty of his back, the triangular shape of him, from the masculine shoulders down a smooth-muscled back to a slim waist and hips in close-fitting trousers. No white coat today—he must be in a hurry. Emma, trying not to think of the sensual all-consuming feelings their embrace in the car park had roused in her, maintained her professional calm, noting down the patient's blood-pressure and pulse that was snapped out in a staccato burst during the examination. He straightened his back and looked down into Mrs Calby's pale lined face.

Suddenly his voice was very gentle. 'Do you think you could stand yet another trip to X-ray? I'm afraid I need to see the state of your lungs today, and get you started on stronger antibiotics.'

The patient spoke gratefully, her pale eyes showing the strain of her illness, but also the hope she placed in her surgeon. 'Whatever you say, Mr Warwick. They'll soon be getting to know me down there.'

'Sister, get the porters to take her down in her own bed. I don't want her in a chair—it might be a bit chilly in the corridor.

'Yes, sir.' Sir. . .he had been Simon on Saturday. But that was Saturday, and Emma had made up her mind that, however charming he appeared to her again, he was a married man, and she would be plain silly to allow herself to be drawn into her orbit against her will. Simon himself ought to have more thoughtfulness.

When he had satisfied himself that there were no pressing problems, Simon expressed himself ready for a more leisurely round of the patients he had operated on last week. Emma had already laid out their case-notes, and the remarks on their charts made by the night sister. Just then the telephone in the ward station shrilled. 'Go and get it, Sister.' He might have been ordering a servant.

'Hello? Orchard Ward. Sister Sandiford speaking.'

'Hello, Sister. Do you have Mr Warwick with you? This is Bill Kenyon on Park Hall Wing. It's urgent, I'm afraid. One of my patients appears to have had a silent coronary.'

'I'll get him for you.' Emma relayed the message quietly, and noticed that Simon covered the length of the ward in just a few of his long strides.

'Hello, Bill? Yes, Simon here. Trouble?' He listened

to the caller for a while. 'Have you tested the enzymes? Good. Yes—I think we can find him a bed. In fact we're going to have to. Sure, Bill, I'll tell Sister Sandiford to expect him. What's his psychiatric state? Ah, I see. . . OK, no problem. And thanks for last week, Bill. I appreciated it a lot.'

Jerry Green and Emma walked back to the ward station in the middle of Orchard Ward. Emma said to Simon, who was standing thoughtfully by the phone, 'Admission?'

'Yes.' Then as an afterthought he added, 'Please. Have you a side-room free? This chap's coming down from the psychiatric wing—depression and paranoia. Bill Kenyon will come over with him and deal with his medication. We're just to get some cardiac investigations done.'

Emma had never done more than a few weeks of psychiatric nursing. 'They couldn't spare a nurse as well?'

Simon paused, then looked down at her with a ghost of a smile. 'Don't worry, his mental problems are being treated—you'll see. You'll manage fine.'

Feeling slightly better at Simon's altered tone and comforting words, Emma became businesslike again. 'I'd better have his name and hospital number, then.'

'The name is Gareth Price. The number will be on his file. They're sending it over with him.'

She nodded, and called one of the nurses to prepare a bed for an admission. To Simon she said conversationally, 'You seem to know this Dr Kenyon well.'

'Quite well,' replied Simon steadily. 'He's a friend of my wife's'

Emma drew in a breath, but silently. Jerry Green wasn't in earshot, but she wasn't going to comment on this, the first time he had mentioned his wife in a conversation. Mrs Warwick must work in psychiatry, then. Doctor? Or nurse? Whatever she was, he had now acknowledged her existence. That had to be a good thing. It meant there would be no more cosy little drinks together—and certainly no more exaggerated compliments. Emma told herself she was glad. But as she walked along the ward to make sure the side-room was ready she knew her feet were fractionally less brisk than they had been first thing that morning.

Gareth Price was brought up on a trolley. He was conscious, and greeted Emma politely. She was slightly taken aback by his sheer youthful good looks. The young man could only be about her own age, and as he lay casually against his pillows, with shining red-gold curls catching the autumnal sunshine, he looked like a film star, with clear greenish eyes and a clean-cut nose and chin. Poor chap, to have other problems as well. But with a secret smile Emma knew she would have no difficulty in getting her nurses to look after him. She stood back to allow Simon to listen carefully to his heart, before connecting him to the monitor and writing a few notes in the thick file that lay on the foot of the bed.

They walked back to her office together. 'Tea, Mr Warwick?' Emma invited.

'It's Simon when we're together.'

She didn't comment. But the ghost of Saturday night hovered again, and with it the tremor of anticipation. . . 'Tea, Simon?'

'Yes, please, Sandy.'

She filled the kettle and switched it on before saying quietly, 'I don't think pet names are quite the done thing—especially when spoken in the same breath as your wife.'

'Nonsense. Pet names are for friends. No harm in them. In fact, they're a good thing.' He hadn't raised his voice, but that element of steel had crept in. She didn't reply, but made the tea, and handed him his cup without a word. He took it, also without speaking, and she found herself unavoidably forced into lifting her eyes to his. He said, 'You don't know how much good you did me on Saturday. I need intelligent company.'

The blue of his eyes was mesmerising her, but she made herself look away, saying sarcastically, 'You know, that almost sounded like the "My wife doesn't understand me" line. Simon, I do want it quite clear—I really have no time for married men. Last Saturday was a one-off.'

'You make yourself very fully understood, Sandy. But who said anything about anything more than friendship? All I want is to be friendly—and I'd like you to feel the same. There's no threat in that, surely? I don't have many friends, because—because, frankly, I'm choosy.'

Emma sipped her tea to give herself time to think. She was frightened, because his argument sounded so plausible, it was a compliment to her, and she did want him as a friend. He was handsome, he was clever, and he was good company, in spite of being secretive about his personal life. He was also internationally recognised as a great surgeon. It was a great compliment to be liked by him. It was going to be very hard to argue herself out of this. Especially because even while she sat with her back to him she felt an invisible bond between them, and knew that, whether she liked it or not, that bond was not for breaking. There was no way out. To try and exert her independence, she said, 'I'll just go and check on Mr Price. Poor boy—he's not had much good luck, has he?'

'You'll do no such thing!'

Emma paused, her back still towards Simon. In a steady, quiet voice she said, 'This is my ward, Mr Warwick, and I won't be ordered about in it like a servant. I don't want that young man to feel forgotten in his little room. I don't know much psychiatry, but I do know that if he's depressed, then he needs people about him, and he needs to be made welcome before he starts to worry.'

She turned to look up at Simon. His eyebrows were threatening a bad storm, but when he finally answered her his tone was marginally more reasonable. 'What I meant to say, Sister, is that it would better if I came with you to talk to young Gareth. I've had more experience with Park Hall Wing. I do know that they can appear plausible and still have no compunction about acting irresponsibly. Trust me?'

Because of his wife working there, probably. All the same, as they both stood at the bedside of the handsome young patient, Emma was very conscious of Simon's look. It was almost as though he was jealous of her interest in Gareth!

## CHAPTER THREE

IT HADN'T been easy, but over the next few days Emma managed to keep herself to herself as far as the quick-tempered Simon Warwick was concerned. She developed the knack of finding a hiding-place as soon as she heard his voice in the corridor—usually shouting at someone. When she was needed, she sheltered by putting Jerry Green in between herself and her chief, and by making sure she was always terribly busy helping her staff with ward chores whenever there was the slightest chance of ending up alone in her office with Simon.

Gareth Price, as Emma suspected, proved very popular with her nurses. His male model looks ensured that he was well looked after, although he was quiet and subdued in manner, probably because of his medication. Emma encouraged him to talk, knowing that bringing his fears and problems into the open would be good for him. 'You're worried about the possibility of operation, aren't you, Gareth?'

'Not really, Sister. You see, I have good friends with me who make sure nothing goes wrong for me.'

'Friends? That's good.' But she felt there was something strange about his calm assurance.

'Yes, I'm never alone, you see.'

Emma looked deeply into the young man's face, the innocent green eyes, and knew she was probably out of her depth with Gareth. She tried to be non-committal. 'That's good, then.' She turned to go. It might be wiser to have a word with Dr Kenyon about Gareth's condition before she perhaps said the wrong thing and upset him. 'I'll be back later, Gareth.'

'That's all right—I'm fine.' There was just a trace of over-assurance in his voice that reminded her that he was on quite heavy medication for his persecution complex. These 'good friends' he was talking about might be all in his own imagination.

Emma went back to her office, where she spoke to Jerry Green. 'Do you think I should speak to Dr Kenyon about Gareth? I'd like to understand his state of mind before I put my foot in it.'

'No problem, Sister. Dr Kenyon's coming over later today to assess Gareth before operation. You can ask him all you want to.'

'That's good.' Dr Bill Kenyon, the consultant psychiatrist, was a good friend of Simon's, by the affable sound of their telephone conversation. Emma found herself wondering if she dared ask him about Mrs Simon Warwick. . . But no, that would be silly, and it would be unprofessional. If Simon himself did not wish to discuss his wife, it was certainly no business of Emma's. She tried not to think about it. But she kept an eye on the door, waiting for the psychiatrist to come with more than usual interest.

Bill Kenyon proved to be a big, hearty man, with a halo of untidy greying hair and an affable handshake. 'You're new to Forrestall, Sister. Hope you've settled in.'

'Yes, thank you. I'm just a little concerned about your patient, Dr Kenyon. I have to confess I haven't had much experience of pshychiatric nursing, and I'd hate to say the wrong thing to Gareth.'

'You're doing fine so far. He tells me he likes it here, and he likes you.'

'That's good. But what about these "friends" of his? Are they real?'

Bill Kenyon settled his bulk into the chair opposite Emma in her room. 'They're real enough to him; that's what counts.'

'But I thought delusions were dangerous.'

Dr Kenyon chuckled. 'Not all of them by any means. Some are delightful. The first thing you should know about my patients is that they're basically normal people, and just because they have an identifiable problem it doesn't make them any the less decent and intelligent people. Now Gareth knows that his friends aren't real, because we've discussed it at length, and he knows that I wouldn't lie to him. Yet to him I'm the one that's in the wrong, because I can't see his friends, and he sees—and hears—them very clearly. See what I mean?'

Emma responded to Dr Kenyon's infectious laugh. 'I think so! But I still feel I'm treading on shaky ground.'

'Then why not come over to Park Hall Wing and talk to some of my nurses? I'd be happy to show you round, and let you chat to my patients. Some of them are quite charming.'

'I'd really like that, Doctor. It's a part of my nursing that I haven't fully experienced. I think it would do me a lot of good.'

Dr Kenyon heaved himself from the chair and put down his coffee-cup. 'Well, I'm over there most days. Give me a ring whenever you want to come.'

'I'm very grateful.' And Emma felt a little guilty, because she knew her curiosity to see inside Park Hall Wing wasn't just to further her own medical knowledge, but also to find out in which department Mrs Simon Warwick worked. She must be a very strong personality, for Simon to remain at Forrestall Hospital when he ought to be at Guy's, or maybe Harefield, using his skill and experience. Just why did his wife want him to stay in comparative isolation in the north of England? And why, too, did Simon not want to discuss it?

'You expecting Mr Warwick today, Sister?' asked Dr Kenyon. 'I'll hang on to have a word with him if he's due.'

'I don't——' But Emma's words were drowned by the familiar roar of Simon Warwick on the warpath. She hoped it wasn't poor Rachel again. As Simon stormed in like a miniature whirlwind she said quickly, 'If one of my nurses is in the wrong, do you mind if I deal with it myself, sir?'

Simon's fury seemed to evaporate at the sight of his trim little ward sister. 'What, Sandy? Oh. . .the trouble in the corridor? Only one of the porters trying to push a wheelchair into the wall. Treating the patient like a load of cabbages instead of a sick woman! These people—sometimes I wonder if they ought to be allowed to work in a hospital.' His voice was less irritable now, and he held out his hand to Dr Kenyon. 'Nice of you to come round, Bill. Have you seen young Price? What do you think of listing him for six weeks' time? He'll have to stay in, naturally.'

'Mentally he's ready. No problem. But where do we nurse him? Here, or in Park Hall?' asked Bill Kenyon.

'To be honest, I think he's settled down here very well. It makes sense to leave him where he is until he's recovered from operation. By then, don't you think his anti-depressive therapy can be discontinued?'

Bill Kenyon nodded his shaggy head. 'Probably

could. I'm not sure about the Stelazine, though. Right . . .then I'll pop in every few days to reassess his medication and gradually reduce it.'

'Good of you, Bill. And Sister can ring you if she's worried about anything?'

'Certainly. But she's coming over to do a spot of revision in psychiatric nursing, aren't you, Sister Sandiford? You can keep me posted about our Gareth.'

'Yes, Doctor,' said Emma.

Simon Warwick turned to her. His voice was steely. 'I don't think that's a very good idea—you've enough to do here! Dr Kenyon has already said you can phone him at any time if you have a query.'

Emma wondered at his attitude. Why shouldn't she do some revision if she wanted to? What could he possibly object to? She said quietly, 'It would be in my own time, Mr Warwick.'

He realised he must have sounded unreasonable. Looking from Dr Kenyon back to Emma, he muttered something about some people being too keen for their own good, and sent her in search of Jerry Green. Emma walked quickly along to the ward, wondering why Simon Warwick didn't want her to meet his wife.

Park Hall Wing was set apart from the rest of the hospital, in a leafy glade, where the gardens had once been landscaped by a former titled owner of the grand house that was now Forrestall Hospital. Its patients could wander along avenues of cypress and beech, or lounge on lawns that used to be home to peacocks and marble statuary. There was an impressive stone lodge at the back entrance that was clearly now being lived in. Washing hung in the garden, and a collie dog lazed on the step in the late autumn afternoon sunshine.

The entire atmosphere was peaceful, and Emma was impressed by the way the cheerful Bill Kenyon had stamped his own benign character on his staff, so that they spoke quietly and respectfully to the patients, and maintained a dignified but relaxed attitude that encouraged informality and security. Emma was sure this peace and gentleness must be of great benefit to curing troubled minds. She made her way in through the high wooden doors, and followed the signs that pointed towards Dr Kenyon's room.

'He won't be long.' His secretary was at work on a small word processor. 'He's just finishing with a group of students. Would you like to sit in with them?'

'No, thanks, not just yet,' said Emma. 'I think I ought to read up a bit more first.'

'Then make yourself comfortable in his room—there's a good selection of the latest journals and textbooks.'

'Thank you very much.' Emma wandered in through the open door, and picked up a journal that lay open at an article entitled 'Alzheimer's Disease and Nutrition'. But her attention was taken by a pile of notepaper on which were printed the names of all the staff in Park Hall Wing. She picked up the top piece and scanned it eagerly. Medical staff included two consultants, two registrars and four SHOs. Feeling like a schoolgirl peeking at some future exam answers, Emma ran her finger down the list and read all the surnames. There was no 'Warwick' among the medical staff. She scanned the list of trained nurses. Again, there was no 'Warwick' listed. If Simon's wife was a nurse, she must surely be fully trained. Perhaps she was in the physio department? Wherever she was, Emma was disappointed not to have tracked her down.

Her face feeling warm with embarrassment, she

pushed the list away. She ought not to be so nosy. Yet she couldn't help her own feelings, and she had to admit to herself that her irascible chief had carved himself a very secure place in her heart. Not that she loved him—oh, dear, no. They were just good friends. . . What else could they possibly be, when he was a married man? As she sat and waited for the pinkness in her cheeks to subside, she had a sudden brainwave. Of course—his wife would be working under her maiden name! No wonder there was no mention of a 'Warwick' working in this wing. She wouldn't want to pull rank by using her married name.

Bill Kenyon came back, and seemed delighted to take her on a tour of his wards. Emma showed a great interest in all he showed her, and an even greater interest in all nurses who wore wedding-rings. Could any of these friendly women be the one Simon Warwick had given up fame and fortune for? Nice and kindly though they were, Emma met no one who stood out as exceptionally pretty or noticeably strong-minded. How she wished she had never come. She felt like a spy. And if by any chance Mrs Warwick did work there, she might wonder why Simon's ward sister was taking such an interest in psychiatry.

'Well, do you think it worthwhile coming, Sister Sandiford?' Dr Kenyon had given up his time generously, and Emma thanked him very much. He went on, 'I'm always pleased to see such keenness in staff from other specialities.'

'It's because I'm nursing Gareth,' Emma lied. 'I'm not really a workaholic!'

'Whatever the reason, I'm sure it will be a help to you in your day-to-day work. Well, don't forget, I live more or less on the premises, so pop in any time.'

'On the premises?' she queried.

'Well, I've a cottage down the road.'

'You don't live in that lovely Lodge, do you? The one with the collie dog?'

Bill Kenyon chuckled. 'No, no, Sister—the Lodge belongs to your chief. Simon and Liz Warwick live there.'

Liz, Liz, Liz. The name went round and round in Emma's head as she walked back to the car park. Now that the woman had a name, it made Emma's infatuation with Simon seem even more wrong, and she drove away fiercely, her foot on the accelerator as she negotiated the hospital gates, making her tyres squeal like a racing driver. Oh, how wrong she had been to pry into his affairs. Now she was paying the price by feeling guilty and ashamed. Yet what had she done? There had only been one kiss. One kiss—yet it had been the sweetest and most potent kiss of her life. Sweeter than wine. . .

It was almost dark now. There was no wind, and the evening brought with it the first hint of early frost, with the stars twinkling brightly and clearly above her. She slowed down as she reached the bend in the road where the Pendle Inn nestled, its lights welcoming, and the flicker of the log fire beckoning, inviting. It would do no harm to stop and have a glass of shandy in that friendly snug. Her mother wouldn't be home from shopping with Beryl, and Emma didn't fancy sitting in an empty house, or cooking a lonely supper.

There was no one in the bar except a couple of farmers discussing sheep prices. Arthur, the landlord, knew her now, and greeted her cheerfully. She took her drink to the corner table and sat in the seat where Simon had sat last time they were there, half hidden by the weeping fig in its wicker pot. There was an almost physical feeling of being at home as she sat down, a feeling of togetherness, of having someone to care for, and being cared for in return. For a moment she was shocked by the strength of the feeling, but then she sat back and allowed it to wash over her and comfort her. The Pendle spell wove its magic around her. Emma knew she ought not to have any feelings for Simon Warwick—yet at this moment she knew very well that there was nothing on earth that could stop her being close to him mentally, spiritually, even if she never set eyes on him again.

The light was suddenly blocked by a human figure. 'Why did you go to Park Hall, Sandy?'

She looked up from a deep reverie, and was not surprised when Simon sat down opposite to her, with a pint glass of bitter in his hand. She didn't apologise. 'Don't you know?'

'I suppose I do.' There was no sign of anger or annoyance in his voice. The cocoon of timelessness was already drawing them together. 'I refuse to talk about myself, so you try to find out for yourself. I take it you passed my house?'

'I saw the Lodge—and a dog. Dr Kenyon told me it was yours.'

'And you want to know why I'm content to live in a gamekeeper's lodge instead of a Regency house in Harley Street?'

'Only if you want to tell me.'

He didn't answer, but slowly shook his head. 'I can't. I'm sorry.'

'It's all right, it wouldn't make any difference.'

'To the way you feel about me?'

'To our—friendship.'

'Is that all it is?' His voice was ragged.

'Simon, please don't make me go home. I want to stay here and sit by the fire and make pictures in the flames.'

He ran his finger up and down the glass on the table, but didn't drink the beer. She felt a strong urge to reach for his hand, and hold those strong slim fingers with both her hands. It was uncanny, the way she read his emotions, knew almost what he was thinking. He wasn't angry with her for prying in Park Hall. She knew he wanted her to find out. But for now she was content just to sit opposite him, and allow their thoughts to merge in a sort of heaven just above their heads—just out of reach.

After a long time he said, 'Gareth Price thinks you're the prettiest girl in the hospital. Did you know that?'

'No. Did he tell you?'

'Yes. He was very disappointed you were off duty this afternoon.' Simon picked up the glass and took a sip. 'You do understand how susceptible he is? You won't lead him on, will you? I'd hate to think how he'd react if you accidentally allowed him to think of you as more than just his nurse.'

'I'll be careful.'

He watched her for a while. 'What pictures can you see in the fire, Sandy?'

She looked into his eyes then, but looked away because the light in them was too bright, too threatening. 'No pictures. Just abstracts, flames and petals and a deep red burning heart.'

She heard him draw in his breath, and knew he was watching her still, but she didn't look at him. He said softly, 'I was wrong. You aren't a hundred years old, you're a thousand. As old as time, and as wise as the earth itself.'

She sat up and wrested her thoughts back to the twentieth century. Smiling at him, she shook her head. 'No, you're wrong. I'm not wise. If I were wise I wouldn't be here. I'd be at home getting Mum's dinner for her, and doing the ironing and watching *Coronation Street*.'

'Go on, then.'

'In a minute, Simon. Just let me have one more minute.' One more minute in their little mutual heaven. One more minute staring into the bloody depths of the glowing fire. The flames were dying now. They became blurred as Emma felt her eyes filling with tears. She knew he was watching her, but dared not look up and meet his gaze. He had a wife, and that was enough to stop her saying what she really wanted to say. She dared not allow their friendship to grow any closer.

His voice was taut suddenly. 'God! I don't think I can stand it.' She looked up, startled, as Simon stood up, crashing his chair back, and edged his way between the tables to the door. In a moment he had gone, and she felt bereft as a widow. She looked at his pint glass, and reached out to touch it where his fingers had been. The two farmers stopped their chat, and looked curiously at Emma for a moment.

She wanted to explain that she had done nothing wrong. What was wrong with chatting to a colleague over a drink? But as she stood up and fastened her coat she felt as exhausted as though she had done a full day's work. They had only sat opposite one another. They hadn't even touched. Yet she felt as though she had been through a huge and momentous experience. As though they had communicated secret and wonderful thoughts to each other, had visited other places, places that only the two of them knew about.

Next morning she felt completely normal again in the ward. The white-coated whirlwind that was Simon Warwick swept into the ward as usual, and she greeted him with a businesslike smile and a pile of case-notes. It was Simon who seemed different today, his usually tidy hair ruffled, and his manner absent-mined. 'Have you seen Gareth this morning, Sister?'

'No, I've only just come on duty.'

'Good.'

She said, 'I haven't forgotten your warning. I'll make sure everything is kept formal.'

He paused for a moment, and looked around to make sure nobody was listening to their conversation. 'I didn't mean to rush away last night.' His tone was stilted now. 'I hope you didn't think——'

'I didn't think anything. There's no need to say anything.'

'I know that. That's what frightens me—the way you read my mind.'

Emma looked up at him as he smoothed back his hair and tried to concentrate on the first patient's notes. She said lightly, 'Frightens you? Surely the great Mr Warwick is never frightened?' But she knew what he meant. It was weird, the way they communicated. An experience she had never felt before. Yet Emma wasn't frightened so much as curious as to why it was happening to them.

He seemed pleased that she had teased him out of his preoccupation. 'I thought so once. But since you came things are different—terribly different.'

They stood for a moment saying nothing. The day outside was bright and chill, the sky clear and the branches of the trees almost bare, black against the sky. Slowly Simon put the notes on the desk, and pulled her into his arms. She could feel his body hard and taut against her, and hers as soft and yielding as though she had no will of her own, but only wanted to merge with his, the way their souls had merged last night.

Then the sensible side of Emma began to take charge. Her arms had moved round his waist, to bring him closer, but now she made her head take over from her heart. She slid her hands between their bodies and pushed hard against his chest. 'We can't help what we feel, Simon, but we can have some control over what we do.'

Simon moved back reluctantly. 'You're right, of course.'

She nodded. 'Don't let it happen again. Never ever, Simon—please?'

'I know you're talking sense. I know very well. I'll do my best.'

'Thank you.' But she knew that the spirit of the Inn had moved into the hospital now. Neither of them would be safe. It was fortunate that the junior, Rachel, tapped on the door and came in with a scared expression on her face.

'I'm sorry, Sister, but it's Mr Price. I think you ought to come.'

'What is it?' Simon and Emma spoke at the same time.

'He's acting funny, sir.'

As they walked swiftly along the ward to Gareth's side-room, Emma asked, 'What do you mean by funny?'

'I think he's—quoting from plays, Sister. Spouting long words, like an actor, like.'

Simon took the lead. 'I believe he did work in the theatre before his illness. I'll go in first. You two wait until I call you.'

Emma heard Gareth's voice, declaiming, 'Prithee, sweet maid—oh, hell, it's you, Warwick.'

'Mr Warwick, yes.' Simon's voice was non-committal, in full control. 'You clearly expected one of the nurses.'

'Only one—my sweet Emma. "Get thee to a nunnery!" "Life is too wicked for such as she." "Frailty, thy name is woman!" "To a nunnery, go!"'

Simon's voice became so quiet that Emma couldn't hear it. She shooed Rachel away while she tried to listen. Simon's face appeared round the door. 'Bring me a sedative, Sandy,' he ordered.

Afterwards, as Gareth slept, Simon walked back with Emma. 'I'm not your only fan, it seems,' he told her. 'He's developed some sort of fixation that you're Ophelia and he's Hamlet, and his mission is to save you from the evil world.'

Emma looked up into Simon's eyes, the dark brows worried as he met her look. She said, 'Evil world, Simon? Or do you think he means his mission is to save me from you?'

Simon stopped dead, forcing her to do so too. He didn't lose his temper, as she half expected. Instead he said, 'Sometimes these patients of Bill's are extremely perceptive. They see things that ordinary people miss. You could be right, Sandy—even though it's totally ridiculous, he might sense that there's something between us. And, whatever has brought this attack on, Gareth has clearly fallen for you. I'd better have a word with Bill as soon as possible. Gareth will sleep for a while now—but don't go into that room, Sandy. Promise me?'

'Of course. Do you think he ought to go back to Park Hall Wing until his operation?'

'To tell the truth, I'd be a lot happier if he did.'

Simon gently touched her hand. 'I can't bear to think that you might be in any danger.' They stood, joined together by only the slightest touch, yet neither wanted to be the first to break the spell. Only the arrival of the library trolley caused them to resume their walk back to the office as though nothing had happened.

# CHAPTER FOUR

'WHY haven't you brought any of your friends home, Em? You told me they were a nice bunch of girls.'

'They are. But—well——' Emma couldn't really explain to her down-to-earth mother that she was going through an intense and passionate love-affair with a shadow. The other girls were just too sensible to understand how raw and easily hurt she felt. If a chap isn't free, then forget him, was their attitude, and it was an attitude that Emma herself took in her normal moments. But her emotions weren't normal. They were deeper and higher and stronger than anything she had ever known before. It wasn't easy to cope with, but she was slowly realising that she must either live with them, and hope that this infatuation would pass, or leave Forrestall altogether.

'You are happy, Em? You aren't sorry that you gave up London for Forrestall?'

'Never, Mum. I'm glad to be home. I've always known that this is where I belong.'

And her mother seemed satisfied with that, even though Emma's sense of belonging owed more to the Pendle witch than to being in her nondescript little home town of Gorston.

It was only two months since Emma had arrived and parked in Simon Warwick's reserved space. Was even that symbolic? She had taken over the space in his heart that was reserved for Liz? The moors were misty all the time now, and the lights of the little inn shone out like a good deed in a naughty world. Winter had settled into Emma's heart, and, though she did her job as well as ever, the moments when she was not working were moments when her heart was sore, and her feelings ragged.

Sally Briggs had noticed. As they sat together in the dining-room after work one day she said. 'You haven't much appetite these days, have you, Emma?'

'What?' Emma had been prodding a rapidly cooling vegetarian pizza for some minutes, while Sally had wolfed an entire helping of chips and a cornish pasty. Emma smiled and said, 'I guess I'm watching my figure.'

'It's more than that, love, admit it.' Sally was not only kind and funny, she was perceptive too. 'Are you missing your London set? Not quite settled in yet? Or is it man trouble?' She saw Emma's fingers tremble as she gave her pizza a poke with a fork. 'I'm sorry, I'm a nosy old thing. But if you want to talk, love, I'm a good listener.'

Emma said carefully, not wanting to give anything away, yet longing to get it off her chest, and share her agony with someone she could trust, 'It isn't man trouble exactly, Sally, but there is someone I can't get out of my mind. I can't tell you more than that.'

Sally said quietly, 'And does he know?'

Emma laid down her fork, giving up the pizza as a bad job. 'I think so.'

'So what happens now?'

Emma had twisted her paper napkin into shreds and now laid the remnants on the plate. 'He's married, Sally.'

'Oh, no! I'm so sorry. Well——' and Sally's natural common-sense shone out of her cheerful eyes '—no use crying over spilt milk. You don't want anything to come of this affair, do you? It's none of my business, I know very well, but you're my friend, and I want you to be happy, just as you were when you first came.'

'So do I, Sally, so do I.'

'You haven't—gone too far, have you?'

'Certainly not. There's nothing between us.'

'So—better steer clear now before it's too late, and not let anything develop.'

'That's exactly what I'm doing. But I've never felt anything like this before. It's—taking me over, Sal.'

'Then,' Sally said briskly, 'if you'll let me, I'll be your agony aunt. We'll start by throwing a party in my place, invite all the best-looking doctors—but no married ones unless they bring their wives. I think that should liven you up a little. With your looks, you'll soon have invitations galore. And the party season's coming! We'll have a whale of a Christmas, and by New Year you'll have forgotten you even knew this mystery man. Anyway, he can't be a very nice person if he lets you go on pining for him. It's just not a gentlemanly thing to do.'

Emma said slowly, 'I realise that. I have from the beginning. It's as though neither of us can help it. I've just never felt such feeling in my life.'

Sally shook her head in sympathy. 'You've got a bad case all right. I can't say I've ever thought anyone worth losing sleep for—but I can see what it's doing to you. You will come to my party, won't you?'

Making an effort to be grateful, Emma said, 'I'll come with pleasure—and I'll help you with the food. Are you working over Christmas? I've volunteered. Mum's going away on a cruise, so the house would be empty anyway.'

'You've done the right thing. When you work over

Christmas, you see so many people so much worse off than yourself, and it helps to make you glad for what you've got. Funny, Emma—when I first met you I didn't take you for the romantic type—too down-to-earth and practical.'

'Maybe I'm the type who gets hit the hardest when it does happen?'

'We won't let it. As from now we're on the Cure for Love as dispensed by Sally Briggs. Never been known to fail!' Sally grinned, and Emma smiled back, already feeling easier for having shared her secret.

It was after six when Abina Brown came into the dining-room looking around her. She hardly ever ate in hospital, but drove back to her family. Emma waved her over, sensing trouble. 'Everything OK, Abina?'

'It's Joe Broadhurst, Emma. I know you're off duty, but I thought you'd like to know. He's been brought in with a coronary. Mr Warwick is scrubbing up now. Says he'll have to re-operate if he's to have any chance at all.'

Emma was on her feet at once. 'I'll go and help. I wasn't doing anything this evening anyway. Thanks for telling me, Abina. Poor Joe—and after he did so well. He was discharged fighting fit only two weeks ago.' She gathered up her coat and shoulder bag. 'See you later, Sally, about the party. And thanks for letting me bend your ear. Say a prayer for Joe for me!' And she hurried out of the swing doors, and back to the ward. She didn't see Sally following her with a concerned look, nor did she see Abina bend down for Sally to whisper a secret in her ear.

The ward was hushed. Visiting was over, and the patients were settling down with their magazines, or watching the television. There was an air of suppressed anxiety. Everyone knew Joe Broadhurst, and knew just how wonderful it had been when Simon Warwick's operation had been a total success. And now they were to ask for a second miracle. Was it asking too much? Emma hung up her coat and went to her office, where Staff Nurse Aindow was on duty. 'Why did you come back, Emma?' asked the nurse. 'I can cope. I'll stay on duty until he comes back from Theatre.'

'No, there's no need. You have a husband and baby to get back to. I don't have anyone depending on me—and I was here when Joe had his first operation. He was one of my first cases. I'd like to stay.'

'I see. Well, it's good of you, if you're sure——' Staff Nurse Aindow did have a family, and it had been hard leaving her baby son with a child-minder. Emma didn't let her waffle on further than, 'Thanks. I hope it's good news. Bye.'

'Sister?'

The voice came from Gareth Price's room. Emma pinned on her cap, and paused outside his door. She knew she had promised Simon not to go in alone, but Gareth's voice sounded normal tonight, and she knew the other nurses were busy. She went in with a breezy smile. 'Are you all right, Gareth?'

'Yes, I'm fine.' The young man's Adonis-like face brightened when he saw her. 'Is it true that Joe's back?'

'Yes, he's in Theatre now.'

'Will he make it?'

Emma was cautious. She didn't want Gareth becoming nervous about his own operation, scheduled for the following week. 'His heart has never worked well. We can only hope.'

'I suppose that's different from my problem. My heart was healthy enough, but I'm a worrier, you see,

Sister, and Dr Kenyon thinks that's what gave me my heart attack.'

He was speaking fast, as though he hadn't had anyone to talk to, and wanted to get his fears and worries off his chest. Emma felt sorry for him—she had been glad enough for a confidante herself, and she let him ramble on. After all, there was nothing she could do now, until Theatre rang to let her know Joe was in Recovery. 'Yes, Gareth, yours is a different case altogether. You'll be fine.'

'I know that, Sister.' He sounded so confident. His 'friends' again! He looked up at her with those perfect eyes. He was wearing dark blue silk pyjamas, and for the first time she wondered what sort of background he came from. Acting, Simon thought. He seemed to know his Shakespeare. He had spent a lot of his life in hospital, of that she was sure. Did that make it more tragic, when he was so beautiful a person? Gareth went on, 'Why don't you wear your first name on your breast, Sister? You don't wear a name-badge like some of the nurses.'

Something made her say, 'My friends call me Sandy.' She knew she ought not to have been so frank, but she pitied the boy, and wanted him to feel comfortable.

His voice sounded perfectly reasonable tonight. 'You have friends too? That's wonderful. I'd like to call you Sandy, too. May I?'

She tried to be diplomatic. 'Well, yes, of course. But only when I'm off duty. I have to maintain discipline among the staff, you see.'

'I understand.' He was gazing at her now, and Simon's words of warning came back to trouble her mind. She ought not to be spending so much time with him. He might easily misinterpret her kindness for something more. And if he suspected Simon of being fond of her too he could become very jealous.

'I must get back, Gareth. I'll let you know how Joe gets on. Goodnight now. Try and sleep.'

'Oh, I'll sleep, Sandy—they've filled me full of pills as usual.' He gave her a sly look. 'But I'll let you into my secret because you're my friend too. When I want to stay awake, I only pretend to swallow them.' So that explained his unusual garrulity.

She tried to be firm without sounding cross. 'You must take what Dr Kenyon prescribes, Gareth. You do want to get better, don't you—get back home to lead a normal life? Do take your tablets. You know they're only for your own good.'

'How do I know that? How do I know what's in the tablets? Someone could easily swap them for arsenic, you know.'

His suspicion was part of his illness, she knew. Emma allowed her voice to become a little more sharp. 'No, they couldn't. No one can swap anyone's tablets. They're given under close supervision. And the poison cupboard is kept under three separate locks for total security.' Having made her point, she softened her tone. 'So do take them, Gareth. Here, I'll pour you some water.' She moved nearer to him and handed him a glass of water. Gareth looked into her eyes for a long time, but she didn't waver, and eventually he accepted the water, produced three white pills from under his pillow and swallowed them. 'Good boy. I'll come back and tell you about Joe.'

'Sandy?'

'Yes?'

'Would you kiss me goodnight?'

'I'm sorry—we're not allowed to do that.'

'No one's looking!' And from a little-boy look he suddenly became roguish, and reached out to grab at her hand. For his slim build, he was nevertheless very strong, and Emma found herself being pulled into his arms and kissed in an inexpert way on her cheek. She was very thankful when he released her then, before she had to call for help, and said pertly, 'Goodnight, Sandy. Be good, sweet maid.'

She stood as straight and as dignified as she could. 'Goodnight, Gareth—and please call me Sister next time, OK? Sleep well.' She watched him snuggle down against the pillows like a child, and although her heart was banging against her ribs at the display of his strength she managed a smile and a confident nod before turning and leaving his room. It hadn't been wise to go alone to him—yet the rest of the staff were busy getting patients ready for sleep, and the poor boy needed reassurance. She had done the right thing, she knew.

She walked quietly along the ward, speaking to those patients still awake. Would there be news of Joe by now? Emma turned into her room—and staggered a pace back when she saw Simon Warwick in theatre greens, his mask pulled down, and his black hair uncombed, sitting at her desk. He was leaning back, the chair on two legs, and he looked very tired. 'Simon!'

He sat up, tilting the chair back into place. 'You're on duty, Sandy?'

'I came when I heard. How's Joe?'

'Surviving—in Recovery. Only time will tell now. The repair I did last time was in good shape, but the coronary artery was almost blocked. I did a graft.'

She said softly, 'Shall I make you some tea?'

'Please.'

'You must be in a hurry to get home.'

'Not really.'

Emma didn't say anything to that. How could a man not want to get back to his home and his wife? She boiled the kettle, and made a pot of tea. They sat in silence with their steaming cups, corresponding without speaking. He was clearly glad she was there. She was happy to be able to give him some slight comfort. Gradually she was aware that he was staring at her, and she turned and met his gaze. Very aware of its magnetism, and the power in those clear blue eyes to trigger a yearning in her that was very hard to control, she said firmly, 'It's time you went home, you know.'

'Are you ordering me?'

'Well, as your friend I am. As your ward sister I have no right to tell you how to do your job. But you can still sit by a telephone in your own comfortable house, instead of my poky little office.'

'Your poky little office suits me right down to the ground.'

Again the deep gravelly voice touched her heart just when she didn't want it to. 'I've told you not to say things like that.'

His well-known temper began to show itself. 'Like what? You're reading things into a perfectly ordinary statement. I only said I didn't feel like moving at the moment. I'm tired—and I just want to be left alone until Recovery phone me.'

'In that case I'll wait in the ward.'

'No—don't go, Sandy.'

She paused at the door. Suddenly she knew she could stand no more of this unbearable sexual tension. His voice triggered a deep response in her that hurt her body and her mind. Her eyes blazed. 'Simon, I'm tired of being used!'

'I don't use you. That's not true. I just—like talking to you because you have a sensible head on your shoulders.' His voice softened. 'In spite of looking like a lost fairy.'

'That's unfair. You ought not to speak like that on duty.'

He stood up then and started pacing the small floor, his hands clenched at his sides. Emma was aware that his reputation for irritability was very well merited. Yet until now, apart from the first day, he had never raised his voice to her. 'Sandy, be careful. Don't turn on me now.'

'I don't want to,' she answered, feeling tears begin to sting her eyes. 'But don't you realise what you're putting me through? Don't you see you're making me love you when I don't want to, when you've no right to let it happen? If you were a gentleman——' she found herself repeating Sally's accusation '—you'd leave me alone and stay out of my life. You aren't free to—to be anything more to me, and you should respect my feelings and leave me to get on with my own life without you.'

When he didn't answer, she looked up into his face. He wasn't angry now. His hands were loose at his sides, the elegant surgeon's fingers relaxed. The blue eyes were soft and caring. 'You said it, Sandy. You admit you love me. You said it.' It was a statement, not a question.

She said hastily, 'No! It isn't true. I didn't mean it. But it might happen if you go on the way you're doing now. You expect me to be here when you need me—yet you refuse to tell me anything at all about yourself. It isn't fair, playing a mystery man, and still expecting me to be on call whenever it suits you!' She was churning out Sally's words again, because her own were too weak and ineffectual.

Simon moved quietly to the desk and sat down again. 'Have you noticed, Sandy, that I haven't ever asked you to come to me? When you have come to me, it's never been because I asked you. It's been something else. . . something outside us both. . .that brought you to me. Don't you see that? Maybe I have a guardian angel after all?'

She was silent for a moment, recalling the times they had met. Yes, they had never made a date, never arranged to meet. It was as though their meetings were arranged for them. She said gently, 'All right, I admit that. I was wrong to blame you outright. But would you please tell your guardian angel to pick on someone else? I'm not made to be a comfort blanket to a man who has a wife and a home. I want to settle down one day, and I don't want my life complicated by other women's husbands!'

He leaned his elbows on the desk, and put his head in his hands. Neither of them spoke, as Emma sat down on the other chair, her eyes full of caring, but her heart determined not to give in. Then the telephone rang. Simon had it before the first note had ended. 'Yes?'

In the depth of night's silence, Emma heard the crackle of the recovery charge nurse's voice. 'He's conscious, sir, and the vital signs are normal.'

Simon breathed out audibly. 'That's great, Mac. I'll get off home, then, but I want to be contacted if there's any change at all.'

'Will do, sir.'

He put the phone down and swung round to face Emma. She was unable to keep the smile from her lips. 'He's going to be all right?'

'Too soon to say, and you know it.' But the relief was palpable in the tiny office. 'The next forty-eight hours will be the worst.' He put his hand out to touch her arm. 'You can go now, Sandy. He's well looked after in Mac's place. Off home with you and have a good sleep. Night Sister will fill you in when you get back on duty.'

'I will.'

'And Sandy——' he began pulling at the strings of his mask, before looking briefly into her eyes '—I'll remember what you said.'

'Thank you.'

'Especially the bit about——' But he didn't complete the sentence. She knew what he meant. She had admitted in so many words that she was falling in love, and there was no way she could take those words back. It made her feel very vulnerable.

She was passing Gareth Price's room on her way out. It was the dead of night, at least three o'clock, and her feet made no noise on the ward floor. She ought to have been tired, but the joy of knowing that Joe Broadhurst had come through the operation made her feel elation. And she was glad, too, that she had made it clear to Simon that nothing more must go on between them. She had explained very firmly, and he had agreed to take her feelings into consideration. Life was going to be a lot less complicated now.

'Oh, Sandy!'

Gareth's voice was a conspiratorial whisper. How on earth had he heard the gentle touch of her rubber soles on the floor? She paused. She didn't want to go in, but as a nurse she ought to tell him the good news, which would cheer him up about his own forthcoming operation. 'Go to sleep, Gareth,' she whispered back. 'Joe's OK. I'll see you in the morning.'

'Could you please get me some more water?'

Emma looked down the ward at the nurse on duty. Rather than call her all the way down, it was quicker just to go in and fill his water-jug from his handbasin tap. She pushed the door open.

'Got you!' Gareth was standing behind the door, and he caught her in his arms. She realised again just how strong he was.

She stifled a shout. 'Let me go at once, Gareth, or I'll be very angry!' To her enormous relief his grip slackened at once. 'Now get back into bed, or I'll call Dr Kenyon!'

'Only a joke,' he muttered, as he pulled the sheet up to his neck. 'Please can I have some water now?'

She fetched the water without a word. Gareth was on bed rest, and she was worried in case he still didn't sleep. 'I'll just get you a sleeping pill,' she told him.

'It's all right, I've got one. I didn't take it.' He grinned in the dim light, then tilted his head like a naughty boy. 'I'll take it now—just for you, Sandy, because you're beautiful.' And he poured a glass of water and popped the tablet in his mouth. Emma didn't leave him until he had quite obviously swallowed it. He looked up at her, expecting congratulations for being a good boy. But then he caught at her sleeve. 'Take care, Sandy. You mustn't trust everyone you work with, you know!' Was he talking of Simon now?

She made a mental note to tell the nurses who gave out the drugs to stay with Gareth until they knew he had taken all his prescribed medication. Maybe it would be wise to get Dr Kenyon over tomorrow and discuss Gareth's growing interest in Emma herself. It could make more problems. Simon had promised to arrange for the boy to be transferred back to Park Hall Wing. The sooner the better.

The car park was dark, the moon hidden behind billowing black clouds. Emma huddled her coat round her and hurried to her car. Her mother would wonder why she wasn't at home, after promising to be there tonight. She drove out of the hospital thoughtfully. It was only as she turned into the road that she realised she had come out of the back gate instead of the front—the back way that led past Park Hall Wing, and past the Lodge. . . There was a light in the upstairs window, and Emma couldn't help looking up as she drove past. He must be there with Liz. His wife and his home—and she had been thoughtless enough to come this way, to allow herself to be reminded of him again just when she was trying to forget him. Why?

It was only when she turned on to the main road home that she passed the inn with the creaking sign, and noticed the smiling face of the Pendle witch cruising along on her broomstick. Emma smiled back at the cheerful apple-cheeked painting. 'I hope you aren't doing any interfering, my lady!' she said aloud. 'I've got more than my fair share of problems just now, and it would be nice to have a month or two of peace and quiet. Tell you what, witch—I'll stop worrying about Simon's wife, if you can fix it so that poor Gareth leaves me alone—maybe even falls for someone else? That would be quite a novelty, witch. Think you could arrange it?'

# CHAPTER FIVE

SALLY BRIGGS' Hallowe'en Party was as much fun as Sally herself. True to her promise, she had assembled most of the junior staff who weren't on duty, and was making sure that Emma met all the personable young men in the hospital. Emma had dressed up, on Sally's instructions, in her most trendy separates—close-fitting leggings and a slinky black top that showed off her trim figure. She wore long beaded earrings, and fluffed her short hair round her face, to make her look more gamine and elf-like. 'Gosh, Emma, you've gone thin!' Sally wasn't impressed. 'Call that a figure? You had a bust when you came here! Here, get some of these sausage rolls into you, woman, before we can't see you sideways!'

A tall young man was listening. 'Don't take any notice of her havering, Emma.' He had a Scottish accent, and a nice friendly face topped with curly fair hair. He wore jeans, and a neat grey sweatshirt, and he immediately took Emma's hand and led her out to dance. 'I'm Mac. I've spoken to you on the phone.'

'Of course, you're Big Mac from Recovery. It's good to meet the face behind the accent, Mac. And thanks for looking after Joe Broadhurst so well.'

'He gave me some anxious moments,' admitted Mac. 'But we got him through. I was fair delighted to see the look of relief in Warwick's face.'

'Yes, he did a good job too,' said Emma, laughing.

'I hear you and he are—'

'You heard wrong! Just a silly rumour, because we work together,' Emma said very quickly.

'Sorry.' The tall man smiled. 'I was only going to say you get on well. The rumour is that you've tamed his bad temper.'

'I didn't mean to fly off the handle.' Emma knew that by her quick reaction she might have aroused some suspicions. 'We're only colleagues, nothing more. I hate to be talked about.'

'I didn't mean to be rude. Only Arthur, the landlord at the Pendle, said you meet there sometimes.'

'We've met twice—both times quite by accident. How people do talk!' Emma heard her voice growing sharp, and tried to calm herself down. 'Isn't it ridiculous how rumours start?'

'I'm glad about that,' said Mac. 'How about coming out with me next Saturday? A meal and a film?'

'That's very nice of you, Mac. You hardly know me.'

'I've got eyes, have I no? I'm not surprised that Warwick noticed you. Even though it was by accident!' he added quickly, as she gave him a warning glance.

'Mr Warwick has a wife,' she said primly.

'Aye, I ken that right enough. But she never goes anywhere with him. I guess there might be a story there. Do you know anything about her?'

'Nothing. But I did wonder why he stays with her, when he could be working in one of the top cardiac centres in London. She works in Park Hall Wing, doesn't she?'

'I dinna ken. But ask Jodie Kelly—that blonde lass taking to Sally. She's in Records, and she knows everybody's secrets.'

'Talking of secrets, Mac——' Here the tape ended, and they moved breathlessly to a corner. Mac brought them both a beer. 'I was asking you how you heard the silly nonsense about me and Simon—Mr Warwick?'

'Och, Emma, this is a hospital! Surely you know everyone knows everything about everybody? Never try and keep a secret in Forrestall. If they can't find one, they'll invent one.'

'As they did with me,' grinned Emma. 'But if they're so good at gossip, it's even more amazing that they haven't managed to winkle out Mrs Simon Warwick. She can't work here, then.'

'That's the only conclusion. But for someone who's not interested in Warwick you certainly are very nosy about his wife!' he teased.

'I couldn't care less. Tell me where you're taking me on Saturday. What films are on?' And she steered the conversation away from anything embrassing. She was grateful to Mac for inviting her out. It made her feel liberated from the shadow of Simon that had haunted her since her very first day at Forrestall. Perhaps now she could start leading a normal life again.

Towards the end of the evening Emma felt a touch on her arm. It was Jodie Kelly. 'Mac said you were asking about someone who worked in Park Hall?' queried Jodie.

'Liz Warwick. And I think I'm wrong—she can't work there, or someone would know her.'

Jodie looked puzzled. 'You mean you know her Christian name? You're the first one who does. Even though the Warwicks live in the hospital grounds, no one I know has ever seen the wife. She certainly doesn't work in the hospital. Someone suggested that he made her up to prove he's not gay.'

'How totally ridiculous!' But Emma knew that by her vehement denial she had opened the door to yet more rumours. She thanked Jodie, and said she wasn't remotely interested in Simon Warwick or his ghostly wife. 'Real people are a lot more fun.' And she conspicuously put her hand in the crook of Mac MacFarlane's arm.

Afterwards, as she and Sally cleared away the paper cups, and scrubbed some of the worst stains from the furniture, she said, 'Thanks for the party.'

'I saw you dancing with Mac,' said Sally. 'He monopolised you. That wasn't my plan at all! I'd got my eye on Big Mac for myself.'

'I don't want to tread on your toes——' began Emma. But when Sally shook her head vehemently she went on, 'I'm going to a movie with him. I like Mac. He's good fun, and he's good at his job. I could do a lot worse.'

'Yes—well, I hope it cures the broken heart, love.' And Sally got down on her knees to moan at a small cigarette burn in her best Chinese rug.

Emma said, 'You didn't tell anyone else what I told you, did you, Sal?'

'About your mystery man? I only told Abina that you had one. She's a sensible woman—and she's got six kids. She's never here to gossip.'

'No.' But Emma couldn't help believing what Mac had said about hospital gossip, and pray that it would go no further.

Winter was definitely in the air now. The trees around the hospital were bare of leaves, but for the conifers, and Park Hall Wing and the Lodge were clearly visible from the ward. Emma glanced at them from time to time during the day, wishing that Simon had either told her everything about himself, or had left her alone altogether. She hated being in this limbo, half in his confidence, yet shut out of the most important part.

Big Mac was a comforting soul, always ready with a wry comment on life that made Emma laugh. She realised she hadn't done much laughing, except with Sally and the girls, since she came to Forrestall. They weren't 'going-out', but he often turned up at Orchard Ward just when it was time for Emma to go off duty, and she found his presence a welcome relief from her constant obsession with her chief.

Simon had been working very hard, operating long lists on each of his theatre days, and often not going home until after eight in the evenings. But he had kept his word, and was speaking to Emma only about business topics. She watched him when he wasn't looking at her, and admired his lean good looks, his skill with the patients, and his sheer breadth of knowledge about his subject. If only he would entrust her with his life story. But perhaps it was better like this. It made it just a little easier to stay aloof.

But it didn't last. He said one morning after a ward round, 'Well, Sister, how am I doing?'

'I beg your pardon?'

'I thought you would have noticed. I've been trying not to shout at the incompetents on the staff.'

She smiled. 'I have noticed. And we all appreciate it. After all, everyone is incompetent when compared to you, you know. You just have impossibly high standards.'

He said shortly, 'You reach them, though.' And then he put down his cup half-full, and left the office very quickly. Emma felt a jerk at her heart, and knew she was far from over her attachment to him, in spite of the cheerful company of Mac MacFarlane.

That evening she walked with Mac to the Pendle. 'I'm due back on duty at nine,' he said, 'but if you've a few minutes to spare I'll buy you a drink, Emma. I need a break.'

She understood the intense pressure of his work in Recovery, how the lives of everyone in his ward were in his hands. 'Yes, of course. Tell me who you have in tonight. Anyone very complicated?'

'They're all complicated—potentially. But I've a wee boy in just now. His parents are with him. Head injury. He saw his pet dog over the road, and ran across without looking. It's an old story. It's a sheer accident, but the mother's blaming herself for not keeping the gate closed, while the father blames himself for letting the dog off the leash. Poor wee thing.'

'Will he make it?'

'He should—bairns are resilient. But it will take a long time.'

Emma shivered in the icy December wind as they turned into the inn porch. Mac said, 'Come away in—we'll sit in the corner by the fire.'

'No!'

'But it's empty. And you need to keep warm—you're used to the warmer climate down in London, not our Pendle Hill gales.'

For once she didn't smile at his teasing. She was feeling the force of all the emotions that had swept over her and Simon when they had sat in that corner. She looked at the seat where he had sat, and was filled with a great sadness. His sadness. No, they couldn't sit there. She chose another table. Mac brought her a beer. 'Here, that will warm the cockles of your heart.' He had ordered a non-alcohol lager. 'Now, lassie, I've got a question for you. Will you spend Christmas Day with me?'

She had successfully evaded any definite commitments until now. This was a surprise. 'But——'

'I know you're on duty until six. After that? I don't go home for Christmas—as you ken, we make more fuss of Hogmanay in our country, and I'm saving my leave till then. Come on, Emma. Two lonely people? I'll cook you a dinner in my place, and we'll crack open a good claret and eat peanuts and watch telly. How about it?'

'Sounds good, Mac.' But while they sat in that inn she felt almost as though she was being unfaithful to Simon. His presence was inexorable. He was there with her, and she knew she could make no promises unless she had made sure that Simon didn't want her that night too. . .on business, of course. Anything else would be wrong.

At ten to nine Mac looked at his watch. 'Time to be away. Coming?'

'No——' she touched her almost full glass '—it'll take me a while to finish this. You go on, Mac. See you tomorrow.' She knew she ought not to stay, but the forces of her infatuation made her want to linger where she and Simon had shared secrets and hopes, while saying nothing in words. It was like remembering an affair, although there had been nothing physical except one kiss in the rain and a brief embrace in the office. She put her chin in her hands and sat alone, staring at the fire.

Then she heard it—the engine of his Jaguar. There was no mistake. There never was with Simon—she knew him so well, while outwardly knowing almost nothing. She knew it was his car, and she knew she must leave before he came in—while he was still parking his car at the side of the inn.

She saw his tall frame through the misty window,

leaning slightly against the wind as he came towards the door. The only way to avoid him was to go into the ladies' room until he had reached his familiar corner, when she knew she could slip away unobserved. She sat there, staring at her pale face and large brown eyes in the mirror, until she was sure Simon must be seated with his pint glass in his hand—that drink that he so seldom finished.

She fastened the buttons of her coat and turned the collar up. Then she slipped out, and into the porch of the inn. Forcing herself not to look back, she started to walk determinedly towards the hospital, wishing she had brought her car. As she passed the window, it was as if her head was turned by force, so that she looked, through that same misty glass, into Simon's eyes, as he sat beside the weeping fig, his noble head erect, and his eyes full of hopelessness.

When she reached the hospital and got into her own car, Emma broke down and cried. She didn't know how she had managed to keep on walking—walking away from him, when his loneliness and need were so great. Why wouldn't he explain himself? Why not tell her about Liz? What was the point of keeping secrets? At least if he told her that his wife had some sort of power over him it would explain his hiding away in a rural hospital, living in a gamekeeper's lodge, and venting his frustration only by occasionally shouting at some poor porter or cadet nurse who had inadvertently done something wrong or careless. But Simon Warwick was a powerful man. How could a mere woman keep him so much in obedience? Liz Warwick must be some woman.

'Abina, where's Mr Warwick's operation list for next Monday?' Always efficient, Emma had grown even more busy as her private life became even more bewildering. She liked to keep her paperwork ahead of schedule, and plan her week around the list of admissions that were due in to the ward.

'There isn't one.'

'No list? Oh, you mean he's letting things slide a little until after Christmas?' Emma knew not many people wanted to be admitted over the festive season, and that usually only emergencies were seen. 'That's fine. So long as I know how many beds will be occupied.'

'Not just Christmas. He's taking his holidays. Didn't he tell you?' Abina looked surprised. 'I thought you knew.'

'No,' said Emma thoughtfully. 'I didn't know.'

'I just assumed you'd know, seeing that you two are so close.' Abina put her hand over her mouth. 'I mean—I didn't mean anything.'

'You've been listening to too much hospital gossip,' said Emma mildly.

Abina smoothed her uniform over her ample hips. 'Even if I hadn't heard any rumours, Emma, I have to be honest. I haven't worked with you for the past few months without getting to know you, love. You hide it well enough in front of the patients—but I've seen you in this room when he's been here, and it's as though you're both in a world of your own.'

Emma felt her cheeks redden. 'I haven't noticed anything. He treats us all the same.'

'Pull the other one,' said Abina, with her usual brand of endearing honesty. 'How come you never get the rough edge of his tongue? Emma Sandiford, I've seen you make a mistake with the case-notes and hand him the wrong one. If that happened with any of us, we'd soon know about it. If it's you, he's as sweet as pie about it. The minute you walk into the ward his voice changes—he stops being crabby.'

Emma said cautiously, 'How many of the nurses have noticed?'

'Most of them, I'd say. If we want anything, we always ask you to ask him—hadn't you noticed that?'

'Abina, that's awful.'

'No, it isn't, love. He's quite used to nurses having a crush on him. After all, let's be honest—he is the best-looking surgeon in the place. It would be unnatural if he didn't cause a few hearts to flutter, even with his temper!'

Emma said, 'There's nothing between us, Abina—I swear it.'

'You can swear as much as you like. I believe you. But I know what I see.'

Emma took a deep breath. 'Oh, well, if he's away from next Monday until the New Year, I've got lots of time to get over it, haven't I?' When Abina didn't answer, Emma went on, 'Do you happen to know where he's going? I mean they. Abroad, is it?'

'Now you know he never breathes a word of his home life. I just hope that wife of his has a nice relaxing time, so that his temper improves when they get back.'

'You think it's Mrs Warwick who makes him cross?'

Abina laughed. 'I know it's my Wally I blame when I come in bad-tempered to work! Who else?'

'I suppose so.' Emma walked slowly out of the office to do a quick ward round. So no new patients next week. That would mean a more restful holiday period. She smiled at the existing patients, and told them that if they weren't home by Christmas she would make sure they enjoyed their stay in Orchard Ward.

'Am I goin' home, Sister?' Joe Broadhurst was sitting up and smiling. 'I realise I've been through a bad patch, and I'm willin' to do as I'm told, you know.'

Emma sat on his bed. 'There's no reason why not as far as I know, Joe. You've done very well after the operation. You could be going home soon to convalesce—but I wanted to ask you about who's at home to look after you. Your wife might find it a bit too much, you being a big fellow.'

'I'm not daft, Sister. You're wonderin' why I come in with a coronary so soon after Mr Warwick repaired the heart muscle.'

'Well, stress is a common contributary factor, that's well known.'

'I know that right enough. But Connie can cope. You 'ave a word with 'er this evenin'. She'll tell you 'erself.'

'OK, Joe. As long as I know you want to go, I'll have a word with Mr Warwick for you.'

When Simon came down to do his ward round, Emma waited to see if he would mention his holidays. But they walked from bed to bed, from room to room and alcove to alcove, smiling and chatting to the patients, but saying nothing at all to each other. Simon declared Joe fit for convalescence, after Emma had had a word with Mrs Broadhurst. They walked back to the office, where Emma began putting the notes in alphabetical order ready for filing.

'May I have a coffee?' asked Simon.

She looked up with a smile. 'Yes, of course.' She put the files down and crossed the room to plug the kettle in.

He said, as though hurt, 'You didn't ask if I wanted one.'

'I'm sorry. I assumed you'd ask if you did.'

'How am I doing at keeping our conversations on the subject of work?'

She smiled again without looking at him, but it was a sad smile. 'Very well, Mr Warwick.'

'But?'

'But what?'

'There was a "but" in your voice.'

'I think you might have imagined that. But——'

'There, I told you so!'

She laughed then. The kettle was boiling, and she poured two cups of instant coffee. 'You're right. I wondered why you hadn't told me about going away.'

He hesitated. 'I knew the news would filter through to you.'

'Well, yes, but I am in charge of the ward. It would have been nice to have been informed, instead of being the last to know.'

'I didn't want to see the look in your eyes.'

'Oh, Simon, that's a bit rich! You actually think I've still got a crush on you! I can assure you I'll hardly notice that you're away, except for the unusual silence in the corridors when no one will be shouting at the juniors.'

He sat down at the desk, placed his coffee on the blotting pad, and reached out to take her left hand in his. She didn't pull it away. He said, studying each finger as though assessing it for operation, and stroking it very gently, so that she tingled from head to foot, 'Why did you run away the other night? I wasn't going to ravish you or anything.'

'I know that. It was—just an impulse. I should have stayed and at least said hello after Mac had gone.'

'You were with Mac? Mac MacFarlane?'

'Yes. Anything wrong?'

'No. Nice guy.'

'Very nice,' Emma said firmly. 'And by the way, you have Gareth listed for after your holidays. Shall I keep him here over Christmas, or let him go back to Dr Kenyon until your return? You did say that you thought he'd be better back in Park Hall.'

Simon lifted her hand to his face, and laid his cheek against it for a moment. As though unable to help himself, he pressed a brief peck of a kiss on the back of her fingers, before allowing her to snatch her hand away. He went on speaking as though nothing had happened. 'Gareth is doing well here now. I don't think another two weeks will hurt, though it's entirely up to you if you want him moved. Kenyon is pleased with his mental progress. The depression is well under control, and he hasn't caused any more upset with you, has he? You've nursed him well. Just remember never to go to his room alone.'

'Does that matter? I did talk to him—the night you were operating on Joe. I thought it right to reassure him.'

Simon's voice was harsh. 'Was he familiar?'

'Y-yes, a little. He called me Sandy. . .'

'And?'

'And he tried to kiss me—on the cheek.'

Simon sighed. 'Don't do it again,' he said wearily. 'I did warn you. I'd better ask Bill to take him back.'

'I won't. But why does it worry you?'

'The last time he was in Park Hall he—tried to assault a nurse.' Simon turned to her. 'It was a long time ago—before he had treatment. I'm not saying he'll do it again, now that he's so much better, but you should never lay yourself open to any provocation. And he's already fantasising about you being Ophelia. It doesn't sound good, Sandy. It worries me. Don't forget, Hamlet went mad over Ophelia.'

'I see what you mean. You did tell me. He might lose sight of reality, you mean, or confuse his own ideas with the truth. I'm not afraid, Simon. I'm sure he recognises that I'm only here to help him get well.'

'Oh, yes? The way Don Quixote recognised that the windmills were giants?'

'Do you think I ought to have a chat with Dr Kenyon?'

'It would set my mind at rest,' he told her.

'I'll watch things — I promise.' And as he stood up she said, 'Have a nice holiday.'

He smiled slightly, and she saw the strain in his lean face, in the sad eyes and the lines around his mouth. He said, 'Come with me, then?'

'Don't talk complete rubbish, Simon. It isn't like you.'

He stood up, and said matter-of-factly, 'It was very flippant of me, and I apologise. I seem to apologise to you quite a lot these days, Sandy.' She turned away and went to look out of the window at the frosting of ice on the grey slate roofs outside, the chimneys sending out smoke signals warning that winter was advancing rapidly.

Simon moved closer to her, and when his arms went round her she leaned her head back against him as they both looked out, beyond the hospital chimneys, to the dark moors out there rising to the dusky horizon. Lights twinkled on, as night fell, and cows lowed melodiously as they were herded in for the night. Gently Simon's hands moved over her body until one encircled her breast and stroked it through the starched uniform. She felt herself quiver at his touch. A button unfastened as though by magic, and his fingers slid inside her dress. For one deliciously sweet moment she kept her conscience at bay, and, suspended in bliss, allowed his warm fingers to move at will, encircling her nipple and sensitively allowing it to mould into his feather-like touch.

But, like a clarion call, Sally's words exploded in her mind. . . 'Not gentlemanly. . .better steer clear now before it's too late, and not let anything develop.'

Even now not wishing to hurt his feelings, Emma moved slowly away, so that his hand slid out and was exposed as the criminal it was. She said softly, 'I'm afraid I'm on the Sally Briggs Cure for Love. It's working, Simon. I don't feel a thing for you at this moment. Time to call it a day.'

He took her shoulders in his hands for a brief squeeze. 'I hear you, Sandy. Next time tell your body what you're saying, because it's contradicting you.' And he kissed her briefly on the cheek. 'Happy Christmas, partner.'

'Oh, go away!' she sighed. But although he went, with a swift wave of the hand, their last sight of each other though the crack in the door was with a smile of love and melancholy and eternity.

She sat down sadly, and tried to make up her mind what to do with Gareth Price. She felt sorry for him, and knew that if he was suddenly bundled out of Orchard Ward it might upset him just as his medication was working and his mental state improving. Yes, unless he misbehaved again, she decided it would be better for him to stay put.

She stood up and went to the window again. The

night was navy blue and the moors were murky grey where they rose to meet the sky. She knew, with as much certainty as though he had declared it, that wherever Simon was he was thinking of her.

## CHAPTER SIX

IT WAS Christmas Eve. The wind roared around the hospital, making Emma glad she didn't have to go out. She was off duty, but had no intention of going home to her mother's empty house. It was better to stay in the nurses' home, where there was plenty of fun, and lots going on. Lots going on, in more ways than one, and she had to keep herself busy, in order the keep at bay mental images of Simon's beloved but troubled face. She hoped that this holiday might cheer him a little, maybe bring him and Liz into a better understanding, and perhaps enable Emma to see him more as an ordinary, workaday colleague, less as the strong silent mystery man she couldn't get out of her head.

Decorations and coloured lights shone everywhere. The dining-room had been transformed by lashings of real holly from the grounds, and a lot of artificial mistletoe by young doctors hoping for its results. The nurses had protested—but only faintly and in fun!—at the sight of groups of housemen carefully cutting out green paper to make leaves, and white plasticine to make the mistletoe berries. 'And they say junior doctors work too hard,' Sally had called out.

And the reply was, 'You'd make more of a fuss if we didn't chase you!'

Outside the wind grew stronger. But inside the residences and the common-rooms the contrast was complete as, instead of the usual silent rush of work and worry, medical and nursing staff walked round with happy smiles and seasonal good wishes and paper hats adorned with wreaths of paper mistletoe. Emma loved the feeling of anticipation before a party, when the room was ready, the glasses arrayed in rows, the bottles gleamed, and the food was temptingly arranged on a white cloth, temporarily covered with clingfilm. She was glad Mac would be down later. She took a last look round, then went to the door to cross the short distance to her flat for a hot bath and a change into her party clothes.

As she stood at the door, she heard her name being called, and saw Sally running towards her. 'Emma, wait.'

'Sure. What's the problem?'

'It's Mrs Kennedy—the angina patient.'

'Is she bad?'

'No, not just now. But you know her, Emma—she just refuses to lie still. She's getting so breathless, because of all the excitement around her. What shall I do? I feel she ought to be moved to a quieter room—but she doesn't want to go.'

'I'll come along and have a talk, shall I? It does seem cruel to move her away from the fun—but if her heart can't stand it, then it's cruel to keep her there.' The two nurses walked quickly back to Orchard Ward, which was sparkling tonight, with silver decorations and fairy lights.

Mrs Kennedy was sitting up, talking excitedly to the lady opposite, and gasping for breath, so that she kept her fingers tightly round the oxygen mask, and took occasional pauses in the conversation to breathe deeply into it.

Emma smiled, understanding. 'You won't miss out, will you, Mrs Kennedy?'

'Oh, Sister, you've not come to take me away?' The look on the drawn old face was pathetic. Taking a whiff of oxygen, Mrs Kennedy said, 'I'm having a right good time in 'ere. It's miserable at 'ome—no one to talk to. Please don't send me away, Sister.'

'It's the last thing I want to do, my dear, but you see how worried Nurse Briggs is. She came to get me even though it's my night off.' Emma sat on the bed. The woman in it was trembling with the looming disappointment of being sent away, and Emma couldn't let her suffer. 'I'm not going to move you, Mrs Kennedy, but listen to me very carefully. You know Mr Warwick's going to put an artificial graft into your artery, don't you?'

'Yes, bless 'im.'

'And didn't he tell you to take things easy, or he wouldn't be able to operate?'

The woman nodded, her sparse grey hair falling around her thin face. 'Aye, 'e did, Sister.'

Emma spoke very seriously, and her patient recognised the warning in her voice. 'If you have another attack of angina, he may not operate. You must take things very easy, even if it means not talking to Mrs Hall so much. Do you think you can do it?'

'Aye.'

'Good. When you find yourself wanting to join in the conversation, remember Mr Warwick. Will you?'

'Aye.' Subdued now, Mrs Kennedy leaned back against the pillows. 'Aye, I'll remember, Sister.'

The conversation had been calm and quiet, and Emma felt she had succeeded. Jerry Green caught her arm as she was leaving the ward. 'Thanks, Emma. Having you give her that little chat is miles better than tranquillising her. I don't want her to be moved either, because I believe her fretting would be as bad for her as talking! Thanks again. Have a good evening at the party.'

The wind buffeted her and the sky was full of racing ragged clouds as Emma made her way towards the nurses' flats. The moon loomed bright and disappeared as though teasing her, as the clouds draped themselves around the sky and danced into different shapes. It was during one of the moonlit moments that she looked across the grounds—and was certain she could see a light in the Lodge. Her heart leapt. Burglars? Someone keeping an eye on the dog? Perhaps Simon hadn't gone away after all?

For a few moments she stood, oblivious of the chill wind, blowing her skirts about, threatening to turn into a gale, and the clouds, threatening to spill their impending downpour. If Simon were there. . . It wouldn't do any harm to edge a little nearer and see if his car was there. After all, she had plenty of time. And she only wanted to see for herself that there were no intruders in his home while he was away. Put like that, it was her duty.

Once among the trees, she was sheltered a little from the wind. Yes, there was definitely a light from inside the Lodge, on the ground floor. She didn't mean to pry. But if Simon was there, perhaps she should invite him to the party at the residence? All the doctors were invited, and most had promised to look in. But what if Liz Warwick answered her knock? Emma decided rapidly not to knock, not to invite them—just to go a little nearer, perhaps to see Simon's face through the window, to see if it had lost any of its drawn, haggard look after a week of his holidays.

The branches of the trees were rustling and cracking

with the force of the wind. Emma shivered suddenly, and decided she really ought not to be here. If Simon Warwick wanted her in his private life, he would have invited her. All the same, she stood for a while staring at the single lit window, and longed to know what kind of a room it was. Had Liz decorated a tree? Had they put up decorations? Another thought came to her—Simon had always known when she was thinking of him. Why didn't he sense that she was there? She felt a sense of excitement at being so near. It was as though his secret was within her grasp.

But then she was suddenly aware of the sharp snap of a branch, a rustling right behind her, the strangled cry of a human being. Turning, frightened, but knowing that someone needed help, she picked her way through the fallen twigs and old blackberry thorns. 'Who is it?' she called.

She could hear, in between gusts of wind, the gurgling gasp of someone in pain. Taking a stride over the brambles, she stumbled over something soft, felt a violent pain in her ankle, and fell across the body of a man, the man who was grunting and gasping to get enough air into his lungs. Wincing with the pain in her leg, she shifted in the damp grass, and reached up to feel the pulse in the man's neck. It was weak. He needed help, and she was in no position to give it. She tried to get up, pulling on the branch of a hazel bush, but her foot wouldn't bear her weight.

She turned back to the man on the ground. In a gleam of moonlight she saw that he was wearing a raincoat over pyjamas. A patient, out without permission. She felt a chill of apprehension—he might be from Park Hall. He might be dangerous. But one look at the limp form convinced her that he was in no position to be dangerous. He needed help, and he needed it now. With all her strength, she reached down and shifted him over on to his side in the recovery position, and made sure he could get the maximum air into his lungs. The she looked again towards the light in Simon's house. She must get there to bring help.

It seemed like a million miles away, as she clung to branches, trying to hop on her good leg towards the gleam of hope through tangled brushwood. She tried shouting, but the wind caught at her throat and blew her words away. She seemed to have been struggling for hours, achieving nothing, when suddenly she felt her good foot slip in a patch of wet grass, and she fell heavily against the trunk of an oak tree, too quickly to save herself with her hands. She knew she was losing consciousness, but fought against it, even as she crumpled in a heap on the ground. . .

Gentle fingers felt her pulse, stroked back her tangled hair from her forehead. Then she was gathered up into someone's arms, and he was saying, 'She'll be all right—she isn't badly hurt. I'll see to her. Get him back to the hospital.' She knew it was Simon. She moaned and started to speak, but he murmured, 'It's all right, love, you're safe. We found Gareth, and he's going to be all right.' She found she was weeping with relief at his gentle words. Gareth Price? She stirred in his arms, but he said, 'Just relax, my darling. He's being cared for. Now it's your turn.'

She had the misty impression of a lovely old-world room, with a sheepskin hearthrug and prettily patterned chairs. There was a log fire burning in a green slate fireplace, and a grandfather clock ticked comfortingly in a corner. Simon, dressed in an old sweater and jeans, laid her gently on a soft sofa, went away, came back with a tumbler. He put his arm around her, and helped her to sit up. 'Sip this brandy—it'll help.'

'What was he doing there?' she asked faintly. 'I didn't encourage him. I did what you told me. I——'

'Shut up, my darling girl. It wasn't your fault. He's cunning, we all know that. He must have followed you.'

'Was it an infarction?'

'Yes. I gave him IV Atropine. They're taking him to Park Hall—he won't be able to slip away from there, even if he were capable of it. It was just as well I was putting the car away. I heard you scream. Thank God you aren't hurt badly. I'll soon have that ankle wrapped up.' Emma sipped the burning spirit, and it gave her strength. She sat up, aware of the state of her dress, and shyly tried to pull her skirt down. Simon said nothing, but brought her a plaid rug, which he wrapped round her. 'There, your modesty is safe.'

'It was my fault, Simon.'

'How could it be? The man's got out before.'

'But I ought to have made sure he was being watched when I left the ward.' She felt the urge to confess it all before his wife came home. 'And I shouldn't have come here. He followed me, and it was wrong of me to come. Simon, I'm sorry for not observing your privacy. I wanted to see where you lived.'

He sat down on the sofa beside her, and turned her face to his with an unexpected open friendly smile. 'You did? And what do you think?' He had a tray beside him, on which was antiseptic and bandages. While he talked, he skilfully wiped the ankle clean, and wrapped a comforting crêpe bandage firmly round the joint. 'We'll get an X-ray if it doesn't go down. I'm sure there's nothing broken.'

She didn't answer his question. 'Could you take me

back to the flat, please? I just want to go to sleep and forget how stupid I've been.'

'Not in this state. Lie back for a moment, and I'll make you a cup of tea. Have you eaten?'

'No. I was going to eat at the party tonight.'

'Then maybe you'd like to have something to eat with me?'

'But—Simon, no! What about—Liz? How can you ask me to stay? It isn't right.'

'Liz isn't here.' His voice was curt.

'She isn't taking her holidays with you? Is she working?'

'In a way.'

She saw then that the strain hadn't gone from his face. 'Are you going to tell me about her?'

He was standing beside her as she lay on the sofa. She could smell the soft wool of his sweater, and the man smell of him that she recognised from her closeness to him at work. He looked down and bent to smooth her hair with incredible tenderness. 'I don't think now is the time.'

'Then take me home—please?'

He said gently, his lovely voice hoarse with emotion—temptation, 'You could stay here. I'll take you back in the morning. You aren't in a fit state to be alone.'

'But——'

'Someone's waiting for you?' He sounded disappointed.

'Yes. Mac was seeing me at the party. He finishes his shift at nine.'

'I see. Would you like me to phone him?'

'I can do it.'

'Sandy, you don't realise what you've been through, struggling through those trees on that foot.' He sat on the edge of the sofa, his body touching hers. 'Look, I'm talking as a doctor now. Will you listen to medical advice, or will you walk out of here like a silly girl?'

'I've been silly once tonight,' she whispered. 'Simon, please forgive me for being so curious. I only wanted to see you—just for a second—to make sure you were all right.'

'I can't blame you for that, love. I've been very secretive, I know. I feel partly to blame for making my whole life such a mystery, yet expecting you to be a friend to me. It wasn't right of me, but I didn't want to lose your friendship, while at the same time I didn't want to break the wall of silence I've built up over the years around my life in Forrestall.' He sighed. 'I believe that's partly why I shout at people, you know, Sandy—my way of keeping other colleagues at arm's length. When I met you, you were the only person I'd ever wanted to be close to. I couldn't help it—you crept through my defences as though they didn't exist—as though you really were magic. It was too late when I realised what I'd done, allowing you into my life. Yet I didn't consciously allow it. It just—happened—to you as well as to me, I think.'

Emma leaned back against the soft cushions, tiredness stealing over her limbs. 'Then let's say it was nobody's fault. Would you ring Mac?' she whispered. She knew that more than anything else in the world she wanted to be here with Simon looking after her. Just this one night. It would do no harm, and she felt so safe and right with him. She wanted nothing else in the world at that moment.

Simon reached for the telephone. 'Recovery, please.' She heard the telephone ringing, and then lifted up. Simon said, 'Is that you, Mac? Simon Warwick here. I have a message from Emma. Now hear me—she's perfectly all right.' A shout from Mac. 'She fell in the grounds earlier this evening, and she's resting now. No, she isn't seriously hurt, but I think she ought to have complete rest for a day or two.'

Emma couldn't hear what Mac was saying, but he spoke for a while before Simon answered quietly, 'I can assure you of that.' He put the phone down. 'Mac wants me to look after you. He wouldn't suspect that there's anything between us, would he? He's too down-to-earth for that.'

Emma said, 'The girls know only that I—have some—feelings for a married man. I suppose if they hear that I'm here with you they might jump to conclusions. But I've never mentioned your name to anyone.'

He stood up again, his brown furrowed. 'Common sense says take you back before tongues start to wag.' He squatted down beside her, so that their faces were very close together. 'But I don't want to, when I know I'm the best person to look after you. Sandy, my dear, I want you to know that I never deliberately set out to make you like me. I honestly don't know how it happened. We just met casually a couple of times, and all at once——' He didn't go on, but there was no need. He stood up straight. 'Look, I'll just phone and check on Gareth's state. I'll need to go and see him later. Let me get you something to eat first, then you can go straight home to bed.'

'I don't want to eat.'

'But you must.' He reached over and took the glass from her hand. 'Lie still and try to rest. I'll soon be back.'

'Do you often cook, Simon?'

'All the time. I'm an expert.'

She watched him through half-closed eyes as he quickly tapped out a telephone number and asked about Gareth Price. 'Sleeping? Pulse? BP?' Then he put the phone down, turned the table lamps low, and went to the kitchen. Emma heard the rattling of dishes and wondered why Simon did all the cooking. And Liz—why wasn't she here? It was almost as though she didn't exist. There was no feminine thing in the room, no knitting or sewing, no magazines or books that might belong to a woman. Yet Simon had acknowledged her existence, and Bill Kenyon had said quite clearly, 'Simon and Liz Warwick live there.'

She slept for a while, the shock catching up with her, to be woken gently by Simon. 'How do you feel?' he asked. 'Are the bruises any easier?'

'Much easier, thanks.'

Simon stroked her hair, his touch infinitely tender. 'God, if I hadn't heard your cries—I don't know what might have happened. You'd be stuck out there—unconscious. . .'

Emma felt her head gingerly where it had struck the tree, and tried to sit up. 'It isn't too bad, really,' she said hastily. 'Tell me, Simon, what will happen to Gareth? Are you still going to operate?'

He nodded. 'Oh, yes. But not in Orchard. He'll be nursed in Park Hall Wing, and only stay in a secure part of the recovery ward for a couple of nights before being taken back. I'm afraid he can't be trusted in a regular ward again, poor fellow.' He put his hand over hers. She was glad that Simon was as forgiving as Emma herself. He knew very well that Gareth lived in a fantasy world, not this one.

She said quietly, 'I was a fool to creep through the

trees alone anyway. Don't blame him. He probably thought his "friends" told him to follow me.'

He kissed her cheek very softly, a feather-touch of a kiss that stirred her whole body with its warm tenderness. Then he went back to the kitchen. Next time she opened her eyes he was saying, 'Time for dinner.' He held out a tray, on which was a plate of savoury rice. 'I hope you like paella.'

'You made this?'

'Oh, yes. It's very simple.' He was watching her face. 'And no, my wife doesn't cook.'

'Too busy?'

He nodded. 'And she won't be back until tomorrow. That's why, against my will, I think I'd better get you home. I won't have people starting to gossip about you and me—it isn't fair to you.'

'Nor to Liz?' suggested Emma.

'Nor to Liz—though she wouldn't care.'

Emma waited, but he didn't volunteer any more information. Liz wouldn't care. . . Emma didn't understand, so she tried a forkful of paella. 'This is very nice, you know.'

'I've had plenty of practice.'

'Aren't you having any?'

'Yes, of course.' He brought a tray for himself, and sat on the easy-chair beside her, and poured two glasses of white wine. 'It's a bit crazy to wish you a Happy Christmas, Sandy, after the hell you've been through, but here's to you, my love, and I hope you feel better soon, and all this becomes a memory.'

'Here's to you too.' She spoke modestly, diffident in Liz Warwick's house with Liz Warwick's husband. . . She raised her glass to him, and their eyes met. He bent over to her as though he couldn't help it, and their lips met in a mutual gentle kiss.

After the meal he made coffee, and allowed her to sit up beside him on the sofa, his arm loosely around her shoulders, protective. Feeling much better, she felt bold enough to ask, 'Don't you miss being among better company, Simon? In your work, I mean. More famous surgeons, up among the latest research in cardiology?'

He pointed to the corner of the room, where a mahogany desk bore a small word processor, and a pile of journals and books. 'I'm possibly more up to date than some of the London fellows, you know. I've more time to read, and more scope to operate. I'm happy here, Sandy—honest.' He was smiling at her concern.

'You don't do much private work,' she remarked.

'I don't want any more money.'

'So you're content with your life? I didn't get that impression when I saw you in the corner of the inn that first time.'

He acknowledged her point. 'What is contentment, Sandy? Do you know?'

'Being satisfied with what you've got? Not crying for the moon?'

'You're right, oh, wise little soul. And I assure you a fellow can be content if he doesn't think too hard about the things he can't have.' He reached out his hand and played with a tendril of her hair. 'How content are you, Sandy?'

She looked down at her fingers twisting together. 'It's all tied up with you. If you're happy, then I will be. But I wish you'd tell me——'

He stopped the expected question with his lips then, holding her head very gently, but holding her very firmly, so that she couldn't escape from his kiss even if she wanted to. She didn't try. This was the only antidote to the fright she had suffered over Gareth—complete tenderness and love. He put his arms around her and drew her close. The kissing grew deeper and sweeter, and she forgot her bruised ankle as her body began to come to life. Then Emma remembered Liz Warwick, and jerked her mouth away from his.

Simon understood. He kissed her neck, and the point of her chin, and his lips were warm and sensuous. 'Don't go just yet, little one. It's all right, believe me. I won't hurt you. Just one more—I promise it will be the last.'

'One, then.'

At her grudging permission, he bent and enfolded her against him with a deep longing sigh. His lips sought hers hungrily, like a man who had lived through a famine, and was only now finding nourishment. He pulled the shawl from her shoulders and began to kiss her body, pulling the dress away from his impatient lips. Pushing it down, he found the hollow between her breasts, and then her nipples, one by one, gently with his tongue, so that they hardened against him, and she lost all will to think or judge, only wanted him close to the length of her body, within her, the way she had dreamed they had been when only their spirits had united. He murmured her name, his breath warm on her skin, and his hands moved over her entire body, pressing it against his obvious and urgent need.

Her remonstration was breathless and ineffective. 'Simon, stop now.' But he covered her lips with his mouth, and she knew she didn't mean it really. Otherwise why was she clinging to him, inviting his caresses and arching her body towards him, needing him to touch her, to possess her bodily as he already had many times in her dreams of him?

They heard the noise through the throbbing of blood in their ears, the pulsing of their hearts as they lay close together, beating against one another. Simon loosened his hold suddenly. 'It's the doorbell.' He leaned on one elbow. His voice was husky with emotion, his eyes misty. 'I'd better answer it—they can see that the light's on. Wrap the shawl around you, Sandy, my love. Lie back and pretend to be asleep.' His breathing was erratic as he stood up and smoothed back his hair. Emma obeyed him and leaned back on the cushions with her eyes closed.

She heard, through the thudding of her own heartbeat, the door being opened, and heard a man's voice, answered by Simon. 'I think she's sleeping, Mac,' he was saying, 'but come in, won't you? I'm glad to say there's no harm done.'

Mac came in, accompanied by a swirl of cold wind. he walked towards the sofa. 'Emma? How are you?'

She opened her eyes. 'I'm fine.'

'So I thought.' His usually amiable voice was harsh. 'You didn't draw the curtains before you started your little games. You're a married man, sir, and this poor lass is defenceless and injured. Don't you think it's unethical to start pawing her yourself? Come on, Emma—I've got a friend's car. I'll take you back to the flat and you can rest in peace without this ageing Don Juan bothering you any more.'

Emma sat up, pulling the shawl closer round her shoulders, appalled at the anger in Mac's eyes. 'It isn't like that at all, Mac. Mr Warwick saved me, and has been very kind to me, and if he kissed me it was because I wanted it.'

His voice was hard and sad. 'I never thought it of you, Emma.'

She said coldly, 'I expect the rest of the hospital will hear of it tomorrow.'

'I'm not one to gossip, and you ken that, Emma. But I thought you had more mother-wit in you. A man with a wife of his own! Poor wee thing, how can I be blaming you? You must have been upset by what happened to you——' Mac turned to Simon, and his once kindly face was purple with indignation. 'To take advantage, sir—to take advantage like that. I can hardly believe what I saw.'

Simon's voice was calm, but intense. 'What you saw, Mac, was two people who care for each other very much.'

'But you've no right to take advantage——'

'Keep your nonconformist conscience out of my life, Mac.' Simon was losing his cool. 'I know very well I've no right! But there are just some things which are beyond all reason, and a man can't live like a monk all his life. Now that you've had your say I'd be grateful if you'd leave my house.'

'Leave her with you——?'

Emma interrupted, 'Mac, I'm not hurt, and I want you to go. Thank you for your concern, but I'll be fine. Please do as Simon asks. It's best for us all.'

'I'll go because you ask me.' Mac looked hard at them both. Then he swung round on his heel, and left the house without another word, leaving the door open, swinging in the storm. Simon walked over and closed it. Then he came back and threw another log on the dying fire. He turned and looked at Emma. 'I'm very sorry. This must be distressing for you. He's right, of course. You must be in an emotional state, and I—I gave in to my feelings when I ought to have had more control.'

'It's all right.' But she felt drained by the scene. 'It

might have been easier on you if it hadn't happened—but Simon, I'm glad it did.'

He strode towards her, and took her in his arms, holding her very close for a long time, his fingers holding her head against him, moving gently in her hair. 'I'll take you home now.'

She said reluctantly, 'I suppose it's best.'

Simon sat up straight then, and gazed into the flames of the fire. 'Oh, Sandy, I wish I could—we could——' But he stopped, seeing the distress in her eyes. 'I'll take you home.'

# CHAPTER SEVEN

EMMA woke slowly and reluctantly. Her ankle ached, and her head was sore. There was a strange ringing sound in her ears, and gradually she realised it was coming from outside her window. As she struggled into consciousness, she realised bells were pealing joyously from the local church. It was Christmas Day! And she was on duty.

She reached for her watch. Her first thought was that she had overslept by an hour, and now only had twenty minutes to wash her face and grab a cup of coffee. It was as she put her foot on the floor that the jerk of pain brought back the shattering events of the previous night. Gareth, sneaking through the trees behind her, collapsing into the undergrowth. . .and Simon, like a lover. . . and Mac, poor angry Mac MacFarlane, finding her in Simon's arms. He must have a poor opinion of her now, but she couldn't regret what she had done. It had proved how much she needed Simon, and how in her need she had turned to him in love. No other man could ever mean the same to her, in spite of it being forbidden and out of the question and totally impossible. If she were sensible, she would have to try to make things different, make a life without him, because he had a wife, and he would not discard this wife, even less speak about her.

She reached Orchard Ward, breathless, at eight-thirty. The night staff were amazed when she walked in, with only a slight limp, the ankle in a shaped elastic band she had begged from Orthopaedic. 'For goodness' sake, Emma, you ought not to be working. We didn't expect you—everyone's saying you sprained your ankle being chased by Gareth. . .you ought to be at home being cared for. Why are you here?'

'Merry Christmas, everyone.' Emma was determined to act as normally as she could. 'Don't fuss now, I'm fine. And I couldn't let the patients down, after I'd promised them I'd be here to join them for Christmas dinner. Look, I even remembered the crackers.'

She went round to every patient, coming back with a pile of cards and presents, which she laid carefully in her office. She sat for a while looking out at the ward, making no attempt to discipline anyone today as they turned the volume of the television up and joined in the carols. Then came the sound of carols in the corridor, as the faithful group of doctors and nurses went, as always, from ward to ward, singing with everyone, and handing out trinkets and mince pies. They turned into Orchard Ward, and Emma went, smiling, to join them.

It was Bill Kenyon who paused in his deep bass rendering of 'Oh, Little Town of Bethlehem' to take her on one side. 'My dear girl, what do you think you're doing?' he demanded.

'My job, Doctor. Happy Christmas! How's Gareth?'

'Recovering well from a heart attack brought on by his own rash foolishness.'

'I blame myself,' Emma told him. 'I should have remembered to see that he was settled for the night.'

'You weren't even on duty, Emma.'

'All the same, I should have remembered. Has Simon been to see him?'

'Yes, he was down at the crack of dawn. Told me you wouldn't be in today.'

'I feel fine. And I couldn't let the patients down.'

The bluff doctor looked at her, and there was a thoughtful smile in his eyes. 'Hmm—Simon wasn't wrong about you, lass. You're plucky, and you're kindly too. Well, I won't argue with you today. Have a happy Christmas, my dear.'

'The same to you. And I'll come and see how Gareth is, if I may? Simon thinks I should only come if you give me the go-ahead.'

'He's right, of course. The lad does have this fixation on you. I'll go into the matter with him, and let you know.'

'Thanks. Wish him a happy Christmas—say from all his friends in Orchard Ward,' said Emma.

'I'll do that, lass.' Dr Kenyon went back to his group of singers, with an admiring look. 'I'm only glad Simon Warwick was on the spot in time.'

'Yes.' He had saved her, that was true. Everyone knew that. But how many people knew how long she had stayed in his house? Would Mac talk? Surely it must be possible to prevent any rumours from starting.

She enjoyed the carefree atmosphere in the ward, so different from the usual tense hurly-burly, and the constant fear that Mr Warwick would find fault and let off steam at someone. Emma wandered around, chatting to her patients, learning more about their private fears and background, which usually there was no time to chat about.

Mrs Kennedy had fulfilled her promise, and had taken part in the Christmas cheer, the carols, the food and drink, from the sidelines. She was looking less drawn, and Emma noticed that she wasn't needing the oxygen so much. 'You've been very good,' Emma said. 'Have you enjoyed it?'

The pale eyes were blissful. 'It were like Paradise, love.'

Emma stood at the foot of the bed, and realised how near she had been to moving Mrs Kennedy for her own good, and thus making her miss one of the happiest days of her little life. 'You've taught me something today,' she said. 'Talking to you was one of the best things I did.'

'I've taught you!' protested Mrs Kennedy. 'You're kidding.'

'It's true. I can see that a little happiness can do more for a patient than a barrel-load of pills. I'll remember that.'

Jerry was standing near by, filling in some forms at the ward station. He said, 'So will I. I'm putting it in her notes, Emma—in medical jargon, "In spite of contra-indications to taking part in Christmas, supervised activity was proved to do more good than harm." How does that sound? Good, eh?'

Emma nodded. It had been a nice Christmas, in its way. It would have been better if she had seen Simon. But his home was very much out of bounds now, and he was unlikely to come over to the ward until his holiday was over. She knew they both hoped no scandal would come of the episode last night.

She didn't go home until after six, happy at spending the day usefully, and she went back to her flat for a shower and a change of clothes.

Later she poured herself a sherry, and lay on the bed in her warm dressing-gown, thinking over the events of the last twenty-four hours. She had never known Simon so affectionate—and Mac so angry. Without meaning to, she had affected them both last night, as well as poor Gareth, who had fantasised about her to the extent of following her into the storm. How much did last night change things in Orchard Ward?

The telephone rang. It was Mac. 'I've been trying to get you. How are you?'

'I'm OK, thank you, Mac. Pleasantly weary.' Emma spoke warily, wondering if he was still angry.

'Are you up? Oh, no, Emma, you haven't been to work today! Are you mad?' He paused, and said awkwardly, 'I guess tonight's dinner is off?'

'Tonight's——?' She had forgotten this date with the young charge nurse, her subconscious mind assuming that after his cold words to Simon last night Mac would not want to pursue his invitation.

Coolly he went on, 'I understand. I hope Warwick hasn't made any attempt to get in touch.'

She bridled. 'No! But that's my business.'

And the kindly Scottish voice, with only her best interests at heart, said, 'Emma, Emma, be careful of that guy. He's bad news—I can smell it. Keep away from him in future, or you'll do something you'll regret.'

'See you, Mac.' She put the phone down, fumbling to get it in the right place. Mac shouldn't have said that; it wasn't his business. She sat on the bed, willing herself to stop shaking at the truth of his words. Slowly the attack passed. After a while she took off her dressing-gown and found a wool skirt and thick sweater. There was no point in sitting around here moping. For a moment she wondered what Mum and Aunty Beryl were making of their Christmas cruise. They'd be in Madeira's harbour today, and the food must be fabulous. That was good—otherwise they would all have been sitting in that claustrophobic little parlour in Gorston, making themselves miserable with the thought that Dad had been alive a year ago. . . She decided she would make a festive meal of cheese on toast and coffee, and then she would go round to Park Hall and ask about Gareth. She wouldn't go in. But it would be nice to know he was on the mend. If she hadn't found him last night, he might not have made it.

She was surprised to find Bill Kenyon himself in the ward. She was confused and bashful when she saw that Simon Warwick was with him. Simon turned and saw her first, as though alerted by her nearness, by that invisible sense that they shared. 'Sandy! You ought to be resting that foot.'

For a moment they looked into one another's eyes, before Bill spoke, and they turned to acknowledge his presence. He said, 'You aren't to let Gareth bother you Emma, regarding his fixation on you. You could do nothing about it. Patients sometimes get fixations on people they haven't even met. But if you want to talk about it——'

'There's nothing to talk about, thanks, Dr Kenyon. The boy had a crush on me and it's no one's fault.' Emma turned and included Simon in her next words. 'It's his heart problem I'm worried about—he was doing so well in Orchard. Will he really be all right?'

Bill Kenyon looked from one to the other, read their eyes, and made a sensible excuse to leave. 'I'll be off, then. I know you won't do anything stupid like go and let Gareth see you. And Emma, I do understand you coming over—you saved that boy's life. He owes it to you.'

She found herself saying, 'Simon saved us. That's my greatest emotion—the relief of being saved, myself and Gareth.'

Bill Kenyon nodded. 'But, with respect, you could have survived a night in the open with only a touch of exposure. Gareth would have died if he hadn't been found when he was.' With a cheery wave, he strode along the corridor to his room.

Simon looked down at her with a gentle smile. 'Isn't it ironic? We're both here on business, yet we're looking as guilty as if we met here on purpose.'

She nodded, and said quietly, 'Maybe we'd better discuss some of your patients, then.'

'Yes.' He pointed to a pile of patients' notes. 'That's what I came for.'

She said bitterly, 'I was such a fool——!'

He stopped her with a finger on her lips, and his voice was low. 'You've been loyal and true and good to me, Sandy.' He stopped, unable for a moment to speak. 'You had every right to be curious about me. I swear I'll tell you everything as soon as—as I think it's fair to all parties concerned.' He meant Liz, of course. He said in his low, husky voice, 'No more secrets. You've earned it.'

'Thank you, Simon.' Tears welled in her eyes. She dashed them away. 'Don't worry, it's only me being silly.'

'No, you're not. It's a natural reaction.' His eyes were compassionate, but he held back from touching her again, and she was grateful for his forbearance. He reached for the files, and said more casually, 'I suppose you know quite a lot about how Park Hall Wing works.'

She nodded. 'I've talked to some of the staff.' With Liz working here, Simon was bound to know more than she did.

'Come and see some of the cardiac patients with me,' he invited. 'You'll be interested to see if the treatment here differs from your patients.'

'Thank you—I'd like to. I can't see the drug therapy

being much different. A heart attack is a heart attack. Angina is angina, whatever ward of the hospital you're in.'

He was opening the top file and saying, 'Now I'd like you to tell me how you'd manage this patient. She's had ischaemic heart disease for years, but only recently—' when a young nurse appeared in the corridor, pushing a small trolley full of vases of flowers she had taken to get clean water. She greeted the consultant politely, and smiled at Emma as she passed. As soon as she had gone, they looked at one another again, each feeling the guilt and the sadness of loving someone one ought not to love. A single daffodil had fallen from the trolley, and Simon bent to pick it up. He put it into Emma's hands, saying colourlessly, 'Winter has to come an end some day. There has to be spring—one day there'll surely be a spring. . . But it may be too late. . .' With a sudden intake of breath, he closed the file and put it back on the pile before turning and walking quickly in the direction of the front door.

Emma watched as he walked away without looking back at her. She knew why he couldn't stay and talk naturally about work. He meant as much to her as life itself, yet there was that bitter barrier between them—that he wasn't free to lovc and be loved. Simon Warwick was forbidden, and for this last six months of her life she had disobeyed her own conscience, as well as the moral opinion of the world. The tears still seeped from her eyes. Inside herself, her heart wept. 'I didn't want to love you. By the time I realised, it was too late.'

Bill Kenyon came out, breezily inviting Emma to come and see Simon's patients. He picked up the files. 'He was coming to see them with me,' he explained.

'He went off somewhere, Doctor—I expect he'll soon be back.' She tried to be breezy too.

He looked grave suddenly, but his natural optimism and his untidy mane of hair gave him a comforting appearance in spite of her misery. 'I think you should call me Bill.'

'If you say so.'

He cleared his throat. 'I wanted to have a chat, Emma. Now I'm not a fool. Simon Warwick has said nothing at all to me about you. But I've been a doctor for twenty-five years, and I've learnt to read between the lines. You and Simon have landed yourselves in love, haven't you?'

'Yes.'

'Thank you for being so frank.'

'But—there's nothing—wrong between us.'

'Hmph! In a way it might be better if there was. It would be easier to get over it.'

'I'll never get over it.'

He gave a crooked smile. 'But you know you must. He'll never divorce Liz. Unless you want to destroy him.'

'I think I knew that. I wasn't going to ask him to.'

'So what do you think we can do about it, Emma? Would it be better if you asked to be transferred to a different ward?'

'Better? I never thought about it.'

'I'll leave it with you, then.' Bill rifled through the files, and pulled out the one with Gareth Price's name and hospital number on the front. It was a very thick file. 'Now, would you be very kind and come to the ward? I need to fill in the details of what happened to him last night. We can use Sister's room.'

'That? Oh, yes, sure.'

'You certainly have no negative feelings about the boy, have you? That helps a lot.'

'I am a nurse, Bill, and I've been caring for Gareth. I know he couldn't help it—that his actions weren't due to any wickedness or wish to do me harm. So—no, no negative feelings.'

'Good, good. Now, fire away, in your own words, Emma.' They were sitting in the quiet oasis of Sister's office. It seemed a million miles away from Christmas here, and Emma realised she was still holding the daffodil Simon had put into her hands. She laid it down diffidently on the side-table as she finished her story.

After she'd said her final words, Bill Kenyon went on scratching away with his fountain-pen for a few minutes, and the only sound was the occasional distant burst of faint laughter, as the patients watched the Christmas shows on television. Bill put his pen down. 'Thank you. I'm writing a book, you see, together with Simon, on the effects of stress on heart cases, and vice versa—the way a mental problem can exacerbate or even sometimes alleviate physical illnesses.'

'I see. So Gareth's behaviour must be relevant. Well, I've told you all I know.'

'Yes, and I'm grateful.' He paused and sat up straight and said quietly, 'Have you parents close by, Emma?'

'Dad died of a heart attack just nine months ago. I wasn't with him—I worked in Charing Cross. I came here to be near my mother. She lives in Gorston, but she's gone off for a Christmas cruise with my aunt. I'm certainly not going to tell her I twisted my ankle, if that's what you're thinking.'

'Quite right.' He smiled, and added thoughtfully, 'I think you've had a fairly traumatic year all told, Emma. May the New Year be a better one.'

'Thank you. Now, I think maybe I'd better be going. I'll pop in to see how Gareth's getting on in a day or two.'

'Don't forget this.' And Emma turned at the door, to find Bill Kenyon holding out the daffodil. She took it silently, glad in a way that someone understood.

'Can I send Mrs Kennedy down to you, Emma? She's made an excellent recovery.' Mac sounded distant, businesslike. They hadn't met since Christmas Eve, and she still felt the weight of his disapproval.

'Yes, any time—I have her bed ready.'

'And a happy New Year to you.'

'Thank you. The same to you.'

'I——' There was a pause. He wanted to say something, but couldn't find the words. 'Sorry, Em.'

She understood, and said so. 'There's a world of meaning in that, Mac, and I appreciate it. Thank you.'

'I never wanted to hurt you.'

'It's over. Another year's starting, and let's hope it's a good one for all of us.'

'Aye.' They were friends again. But it would never be quite the same. Emma sighed. A good year? Hardly, if things between herself and Simon stayed the same. Bill Kenyon had suggested transferring from Simon's ward, but that didn't make any sense. She loved it here, and she knew she was good at it.

Mrs Kennedy was soon settled in a post-op bed, declaring her eternal gratitude to Mr Warwick. 'He's a miracle-worker, that one.'

'No one better,' agreed Emma, always delighted to sing Simon's praises.

'I heard that.' It was Simon himself in starched white

coat, with Jerry Green beside him, standing at the foot of the bed. 'Thank you, ladies.'

Emma's heart leapt at the sound of his beloved voice. She remembered that she wasn't supposed to know how Simon had spent his holiday. 'Good morning, Doctor. How was your holiday?'

'Pretty good, thank you, Sister, but it's nice to be back.' He bent to greet the little patient. 'And I don't need to ask how you are, Mrs Kennedy. Comfortable?'

'Oh, yes!'

Simon chatted to her for a moment, before moving off to the next bed. He said to Emma, 'By the way, I've arranged to see two patients being referred from outside Manchester. The waiting lists are too long in the city hospitals, so I've been asked to take them. One's a simple mitral stenosis—I saw her in clinic this morning. Name's Grey. The other isn't quite so straightforward, a retired schoolteacher with an atrial septal defect. The lung vessels are sclerosed, and there's a very real danger of right-sided heart failure. Sorry I didn't let you know earlier—can you cope with two extra patients? I've listed them for Thursday.'

'I'll manage.' There weren't any beds, but one patient might be going home this afternoon, and she could possibly use the side-room for a couple of nights. It was good to be busy. It left less time to grieve.

'Sister!' A hissed plea from a young woman who had been admitted for investigation of her irregular heart-beat. Emma made sure the doctors didn't need her, before bending to hear what the patient wanted. 'It's my chest, Sister—I've got a terrible pain.'

'Pain? Where exactly? What kind of pain?' Emma knew without panicking how to question a heart patient, although naturally a heart attack was always at the back of her mind.

'Like a stitch. Just here.' The woman looked frightened, her eyes were large and bright.

'Then it isn't a heart attack. Calm down, my dear. I'll call Mr Warwick.' Emma reached to take the young woman's pulse. It was fast and irregular again, and Emma reassured the patient while she went to get Simon. 'Miss Hale—chest pains and fast pulse. Doctor, her eyes looked suspiciously prominent today. Did she have her thyroxine checked?'

He smiled. 'Coming. And yes, she had a blood test, but the results aren't out yet.' He strode to Miss Hale's bedside and took out his stethoscope. After examination he said to the patient, 'Sister was quite right—your heart's fine. The trouble's with your thyroid—we'll have you transferred to the medical ward as soon as possible, but I'll have a word with Dr Clegg now so that we can start you on the right medication straight away, as soon as we get your blood test results.' To Emma he said quietly, 'Phone Pathology and get the thyroxine results a.s.a.p., and make sure we have some Carbimazole ready. It looks as thought we've found a bed here for Mrs Grey after all—this isn't a heart case. Her fibrillation is due to an over-active thyroid, and she'll be right as rain within a few days. Thanks, Sandy. And well done for spotting the exophthalmos. It's mild, but it definitely helps in the correct diagnosis.'

After work that evening Emma sat for a while, leafing through the patients' notes. It had been a busy day, but working alongside Simon wasn't like work. It was a pleasure in spite of the pain of loving him. She knew she would rather endure this sweet pain than transfer to another ward, and never see him in such close proximity.

Before going home, she crossed the grounds to Park Hall, to see how young Gareth was getting on. It was a cool grey evening, damp and clammy, the most miserable of weather that did nothing for her mood. Bill Kenyon was in the middle of a lecture to a group of students, and Emma silently drew back from his room and closed the door. The secretary said, 'He'll be free in about five minutes, Emma. Want to wait?'

'All right, as I'm already here. I've nothing else to do.' She walked idly along the corridor, knowing that she was hoping Simon might be here also—Park Hall was on his way home. The door of the day-room was ajar, and the sound of voices came from the television set. Emma pushed the door open. The room was empty but for a little old woman dressed in a simple smock, with long grey hair tied back with a ribbon. She was staring out of the barred window. Emma spoke gently, so as not to alarm her. 'Hello,' she smiled, 'I'm Emma.' She went in and looked encouragingly at the woman.

The patient turned round, and Emma saw with a shock that she wasn't old at all. Her face was clear and pale, with no sign of wrinkles. In fact, she was almost pretty, except for the blankness. There was a face there, with large pale blue eyes in dark sockets, and there was a slight body that looked as though it might blow away, but behind it there was nothing—no personality, no feelings, no cares. 'Hello,' she said tonelessly. 'I'm Liz.'

Emma felt her heart somersault. Her voice came out jerkily, as she tried to be normal. 'Nice to meet you. Are you—a patient on this ward?'

'I don't know.'

Emma felt a surge of pity for her then. Trying to look

on her as a patient, and not as Simon's wife, she asked, 'Have you any relatives who come and see you?'

'No.'

She couldn't be Simon's wife, then. Emma looked around the little room. There was a TV set, and plenty of magazines. But Liz sat there like a statue, staring into space, taking no interest in anything. Emma said, 'This is a nice room.'

Liz turned and looked into her face, uncomprehending. 'Who are you?'

'My name's Emma.'

'Oh. I'm Liz.'

Emma bit her lip. 'Hi, Liz. Shall I put the television on?'

'Yes.'

'Can you tell me anything about yourself? Or don't you want to talk?'

Liz was still looking at her, and her pale eyes might have been blind, for all the interest they took in her surroundings. 'Yes,' she said. 'My name's Liz.'

'Liz who?'

'Don't know'

'Oh, Liz. . .' Emma looked searchingly at this wraith that she knew in her heart must be Simon's wife, and felt herself dissolving into tears. All this time she had wondered what kind of person Liz Warwick could be, what sort of hold she had over her husband. Never had she once thought that his tie to his wife was one of pity and duty, that Liz herself neither wanted nor demanded him to be faithful. Emma's admiration for Simon had never been greater. She looked back at the living ghost that was Liz Warwick, and envied her, because she possessed such a giant of a man—till death did them part. . .

# CHAPTER EIGHT

DR BILL KENYON was alone in his room, shuffling papers together and putting them away. Emma stood for a moment in the doorway, not really wanting to be noticed, because she didn't want to hear the truth—and yet knowing she couldn't leave tonight without being sure in her own mind that there were no more questions left to be answered. Somehow she didn't want the pale sad woman to be Liz Warwick—yet in her bones she knew she was.

'Oh, it's you, Emma! You startled me. And how are you feeling today, my dear? You look a bit wan. Must be this rotten weather, eh?'

She sat down, so that her face was more on a level with his. It was important to see his expression when she asked him what she had to ask. 'Bill, I went to the day-room—I hope you don't mind.'

'Course I don't. Sorry I was tied up with the students, but I know you won't do anything foolish. Gareth's keeping up his improvement very nicely, if that's what you came for.'

She nodded, subdued. 'I did, Bill. But may I ask you something else?'

'Of course. That's why I'm here.'

'Who is the pale woman in the smock with the big eyes?'

He wasn't expecting the question. But she saw that he understood its importance to her. He said quietly, sympathetically, 'She was in the day-room again? They really must keep a better eye on her.' He paused, and met Emma's intense gaze. 'Yes, my dear, she's Simon's wife.'

Although she knew it, Emma felt as though she had been punched very hard, hearing the words spoken so candidly. She swallowed and, trying to keep her voice steady, she asked, 'And can you tell me what's the matter with her?'

He thought for a moment before replying. 'I can, naturally. I suppose it would be best to level with you now. It's—a very tragic tale, I'm afraid. There's nothing the matter with her physically. She suffered from meningitis—only a month or so after they were married. A virulent strain. They thought she might not survive. It might have been better if she hadn't. . . But she did recover, nursed so lovingly by her husband—but it was soon clear that she'd completely lost her memory. It was totally destroyed by the virus. To Liz, there's only "now". "Before" and "after" are beyond her comprehension.'

Emma could feel only pity for the woman, forgetting for a moment her own tragic involvement. 'Poor soul. Poor lost soul. Does she live here?'

Bill Kenyon nodded. 'During the day, or when Simon is very tired. You see, she has to be looked after full-time. She has no fear of fire, or electricity. She'll wander, walk under a bus, cut herself on the wire fence in the grounds. She once strayed on to the moors, when a pheasant shoot was taking place. How she escaped that we'll never know.'

'And the rest of the time she stays in the Lodge with Simon?'

'Yes. He's devoted his life to her.'

'He cooks for her too?'

'Every day.'

Emma looked down, and found she was shredding the magazine she had been holding. 'And the evenings when he goes to the inn?'

'I go over and sit with her. Sometimes my wife comes too. It's a bit like baby-sitting, really, poor lady.'

'Does she know anyone?' The saga was tearing at Emma's heart, but she wanted to know every single detail, now that she had started.

'She knows her name and Simon's. But not her surname—I think she mixes it up with her maiden name, so decides not to try and remember. If you told her your name, she'll have forgotten it within a few seconds.'

'I noticed that. It's just—so cruel, Bill.'

'Yes, that's the word, Emma. Even more since you came on the scene, and the possibility of a little human happiness crossed Simon's path.'

Emma felt herself blushing. 'Did he tell you anything about me, then?'

'No, he's never said a word. But he changed. There was a light in his eye again, and a spring to his step. It wasn't hard to guess he'd found someone else. Someone he could talk to, if nothing else.' He looked gravely at her, his usual twinkle quite absent. 'So you see, Emma, why Simon didn't tell you, and why he never wants anyone to know.'

'And why,' said Emma slowly and very sadly, 'he'll never leave her, even though she wouldn't know anything about it. He's some guy.'

'As you say, Emma, he's some guy. And does it make you feel a little better about being his friend, now that you know it isn't hurting Liz?'

'I'm not sure,' Emma responded. She knew she

wanted Simon for herself, and having met the woman he married, the woman he had remained faithful to for so long, she felt curiously pushed out and uninvolved. 'I think I feel worse, as though I'm taking advantage of her misfortune.'

'You didn't do it on purpose. I suppose you had to find out in the end. I'm sorry, Emma. Life just isn't being very fair to you just now. But you have the guts to take life on at its own game. I know that whatever happens you'll come out on top of it.'

'Thanks, Bill. I'm not as sure as you, but I won't give up on it if I can help it.'

'That's my girl.' There was a crumb of comfort in Bill's fatherly attitude. But only a crumb.

Mrs Grey with the mitral stenosis, and the retired schoolmistress with the atrial septal defect, were admitted next morning, and Emma soon realised that these two were admirable material for the book Simon and Bill were collaborating on. Mrs Grey had the simpler, treatable problem, but she was a worrier, and her anxiety was causing her a lot more trouble than her medical condition. The teacher, Mrs Phipps, with the small hole in her heart needing urgent operation, on the verge of heart failure and its associated problems, calmly and with a dry wit accepted her lot, and endeavoured to cheer up the other woman rather than dwell on her own illness.

Simon had already come to the same decision. 'I'll be operating on Mrs Phipps tomorrow. Just look at her! You'd think she was going to the supermarket for her weekly groceries, instead of having an operation that might not be a success.'

Emma said staunchly, 'She has you for a surgeon, that's why!'

'You know as well as I do that it isn't just the hole in the heart. The associated blood vessels are affected quite seriously, and I'm really not sure what we can do about those. If only she'd had treatment earlier. You see, this type of patient is used to putting up with discomfort—she probably never even complained that she felt unwell.'

'Well, I think her husband depends on her a lot,' Emma pointed out.

'Exactly—she didn't want to upset him! Sometimes a little selfishness is necessary in life.'

Simon was smiling as he spoke, but Emma couldn't get the wraith of Liz Warwick out of her mind, and she said without thinking, 'Some people are too good for their own good.'

He looked hard at her. 'You said that very seriously. Anything wrong?'

'No, no, nothing!' she snapped, turning to pick up Mrs Phipps's notes. 'Here, you'd better keep them in that side-drawer, so that your secretary can add her to her list of patients for your book.'

'If I weren't in a hurry, I'd want a word with you.'

Emma said coolly, 'Better not. Now isn't the time.' And she turned swiftly to carry on settling the two new patients in their beds, and dismissing their relatives with soothing words of reassurance.

Mrs Grey, puffy with weeping, didn't want her niece to leave her. 'She works in the hospital, Sister Sandiford. Can't she stay with me until she has to go to work?'

Emma looked at the niece, a striking dark-haired girl of about twenty-four. 'I'm Caroline Brett—I'm helping

Dr Kenyon and Mr Warwick with their research for their book,' said the girl. 'I have qualifications in mental health.' She added, 'I think I saw you in Park Hall last week—about Gareth Price.'

Emma nodded. 'I see. Well, as your aunt is in such a state of nerves, you can possibly be quite a help to her.'

'Thanks, Sister.' Caroline settled herself and her glamorous fake fur coat beside the bed again. She turned as Emma passed by, and said in a low voice, 'Nice to be working with the best-looking surgeon in Forrestall!'

Emma didn't reply. Caroline Brett might have been trying to find out if some of the gossip that no doubt was beginning to circulate was true. She had no intention of giving anything away. But she made a mental note to tell Simon to be careful. Women like Caroline could be dangerous.

Before she left the ward that evening, Emma did a quick round, to chat to the patients who were having their operations the following morning. She was surprised to note that Caroline Brett was again beside her aunt's bed. 'I just popped in on my way home,' she explained.

'That's all right,' sid Emma. 'It's visiting anyway.'

'I'm just off, actually. I'll walk down with you.' And Caroline Brett kissed her aunt, and promised to look in before the operation in the morning. Emma didn't particularly seek company, but she was civil to the tall brunette as they walked down the corridor together. Caroline said, 'I know she'll be fine—that the operation is straightforward. But she will work herself up for nothing. I'm glad she'll be first on the operating list tomorrow. That's thoughtful of Mr Warwick.'

Emma was thinking that if Caroline worked in Park Hall she would very likely know about Liz Warwick.

But she decided to say nothing. It was nobody's business but Simon's. She replied automatically, 'Mr Warwick never treats a disease on its own. He always thinks of the person with the disease, and I believe that's one of the reasons he has so many successes.'

Caroline said, 'It's easy to see you're one of his fans.'

Was she fishing again? Emma brushed aside the hint by saying, 'And your aunt will be another by this time tomorrow!'

When Caroline had gone, Emma fastened her coat and went for a stroll in the gardens. She didn't go towards the Lodge, but she felt overwhelmed by what she had learnt, and wanted to be quiet and alone for a while. It was a grey, overcast evening, shortly to dwindle into night, and the trees were bare, damp leaves rotting underfoot. She stayed well away from the Lodge and from Park Hall. She had no fear of walking alone. She sat for a moment on a rustic wooden bench, her hands in her pockets, breathing in the smell of dead leaves, of rotting wood, and the clean sharp smell of imminent frost.

And then she had a feeling of warmth in the sharp grey day, a sense of happiness. His voice didn't surprise her. 'Sandy, all alone?'

'Simon!'

'Shh! I shouldn't be here. But I'm afraid I've been loitering with intent—I did want to see how you were. You said some things in the ward that needed a bit of explanation. Do I get that explanation now?'

Emma stood up from the wooden bench and pulled her coat more tightly about her. He stood, in his smart hospital suit, tired after work, his raincoat over his arm, and looked down at her. She rejoiced in her heart to see him, but she knew that he was hurrying home to look after his wife, and she felt she had no right to be preventing him. She had to tell him now. 'I've met Liz, Simon.'

If she ever pitied him before, she did now. Strong and unmoved, he stood, bearing the weight of the world on his shoulders. His eyes were direct, his quiet inner self hidden. Only his voice spoke. 'Oh, God, how did that happen?'

She looked into the troubled blue eyes, recalling the first time she had seen them, as he berated her for taking his parking place on her very first day at Forrestall. Her voice was soft, pleading. 'Maybe it was right that it did. I'm glad I know your secret, Simon. It will make it easier to stay away.'

'You don't mean that, do you? Completely? What difference does it make? Sandy, Sandy, my friend—now that you know, you should want to help me, surely.'

Her own feelings threatened to engulf her, and she had to stop him appealing to her love. It was hard, but she had to be hard, although, God help her, she knew she was his only hope, and she yearned to be able to bring a smile to his tormented face. Choosing the cruellest words she could, and hating herself for doing it, she said, 'That's a selfish point of view, and you know it is, Simon. Can't you see that I need to make a life of my own? You may be tied down, but you shouldn't expect me to follow you to despair. I'm still young, Simon, and I've got a life in front of me. I think—in fact I know—that it would be sensible for me to ask for a transfer from your ward.'

'As you wish.' His answer was more like a sigh, like a condemned man's hopelessness. He turned and walked towards the Lodge, and Emma ran away, because she knew she couldn't bear to see them together, the devoted husband steering his wife to their little home in the grounds of the hospital. A dead home, and a dead marriage, yet it lived and would go on living.

On Orchard Ward, Emma felt relief, because the patients didn't know what problems she had. To them, she was a gentle and caring nurse, and all her talk was about their complaints and their troubles. Her brow was clear, and her face smiling. She was doing her job, and her job included concealing any possible emotional upsets that were eating up her soul.

'Mr Warwick is coming up with a patient from Recovery, Sister.'

She tried to ignore the beating of her heart. 'That's all right. The bed's ready, and I've put up the drip.' She picked up Mrs Grey's case-sheet to put at the foot of the bed. It had been a straightforward mitral valve replacement—routine to Simon, but an earth-shattering event to Mrs Grey. Emma wondered how she would be, now that surgery was over, and was totally successful. She would have to speak to the relatives unless Simon wanted to, and the only relative so far was the lovely Caroline Brett.

This would be the first time she had seen Simon since she had raised her voice, told him in no uncertain terms that from now on she was going to lead her own life. Emma knew that her first encounter with Simon Warwick on business terms would set the scene for all her future decisions. She heard the rattle of the trolley in the corridor, and went to meet it with professional calm. The fact that the man who had saved this lady's life was the most important person in the world to Emma didn't affect her kindly attitude to her patient, and her interest in the theatre nurse's notes on the operation. 'Nervous, and possibly a strong reaction to the anaesthetic.' That was scarcely unexpected, given Mrs Grey's previous history of nerves. All the same, this patient had been through a traumatic experience, and just because Emma had seen it hundreds of times before it didn't make it any less important to the individual. Emma took over the monitoring, checking the blood-pressure with her own sphygmomanometer, and taking the pulse regularly.

Simon was in the office, writing up notes. She didn't go to him, knowing that he would call her if he needed anything. But he didn't call, and when she eventually went to her office Simon had left it, with notes about the patient left in a prominent position. 'I'll talk to the relatives if they wish,' he had noted. That was a relief. But Emma felt a pang of remorse that he had felt the need to write to her, when he could have spoken to her without her getting emotional. That was something they would have to come to terms with over the next few weeks.

He rang her later about the patient. 'Sandy?'

There was no one else in the world who called her that. 'Yes?' It was hard not to say more.

'Mrs Grey—no problems?'

'Doing very well indeed.'

'You won't need me to come and see her?'

Emma breathed in deeply before answering. It would be good to see him. But she knew why he had telephoned first. Without a medical need, he intended to stay out of her ward. She admitted, 'No—she's doing fine.'

'BP all right?'

'Normal.'

'Pulse?'

'Was slow, but just getting back to normal.'

'Alert?'

'Hardly alert, but rational, and a bit nauseated.'

'And how is she mentally?'

'Thank goodness she seems much less neurotic.'

'OK. I'll leave her in your hands, then.'

'I'm sure you won't regret it.' Her reply was a little personal, but she couldn't help it.

His response was similarly humorous, for which she was grateful. 'I know I won't. Lucky Mrs Grey.'

'Bye, Simon.'

'Bye——'

She had hung up before he had time to say any more. this was the way it would be; working together, but with no contact outside Orchard Ward. And all the time the picture of Liz, her prematurely grey hair drawn into a childlike bunch, and her wide pale eyes gazing at nothing, standing impassively between them. A wicked wife was one thing—an innocent one was too much.

Sally was waiting after work. 'The girls are going out,' she said. 'Coming?'

'Sure, why not?'

'That's great, Emma—we thought maybe—you haven't had much of a Christmas and New Year, have you?'

So the gossip was beginning. 'I only fell over and hurt my ankle. That's not the end of the world, you know!' Emma kept her voice perky.

'Of course not. But weren't you lucky to have Simon Warwick to rescue you?' Sally's eyes were unusually keen.

This was the testing time. To say too little would draw attention to her; to say too much would be very unwise. Emma felt her pulse racing as she sought in her brain for a suitable reply. 'I was lucky anyone at all heard me, in that wind. Thank goodness I'm a good screamer! He gave poor Gareth the right treatment straight away. And me? I was all right by next morning—you saw me.'

'That's great, Emma. So get some gear on, and let's hit town.'

'No problem. Where shall I meet you?'

'The Pendle—in half an hour!'

'Right.' Emma hoped they didn't hear the dread in her voice. But why? The inn was so near to the hospital that it was almost always inhabited by someone from Forrestall. It was something Emma would just have to get used to—unless she really intended to follow up Dr Kenyon's suggestion, and apply to somewhere completely away from Simon Warwick. . . 'The Pendle in half an hour.'

As she walked there, Emma wondered if Sally was already putting two and two together: Emma loves a married man—Emma rescued by a married man. . . There was no identity for the married man, but she knew her friends were pretty much scholarship standard at working out matters of the heart. She hoped very much that they managed to keep their curiosity to themselves.

It was a drab, cool January night, and the Inn fire was blazing merrily. Emma ignored the swinging sign that had treated her disgracefully, all things considered, and walked in with a smile on her face. 'Where's the action, then?'

'We're thinking of trying the new arts centre for a meal. What do you think?'

'Sounds great. They're so new, they'll give us value for money anyway. And we might get info on all the latest groups coming to town.'

'They do concerts. And plays. I'm not sure what else,' Sally said.

'Probably jazz, puppets, that sort of thing. I think we ought to support them. It could be a good place to meet—specially if the food is OK.'

The girls went on discussing what was on in town. They were all grouped about the bar. Emma was in the middle of the group when she felt her voice suddenly fade and disappear into her throat. She stopped talking, leaving others to carry on. But she knew very well what had happened. Simon had come in.

She looked from the corner of her eye, but she didn't need to. Simon had gone to his corner, and the landlord had nonchalantly filled a pint glass and taken it over, without anyone else noticing. Life went on as normal, except that Emma's heart was pounding like a steam engine. 'How are we getting to town, then?' She felt she had to contribute to the general conversation. 'Want me to go back for my car?'

'Heck, no. You want a drink, don't you? We'll walk in and take a cab home. Everyone ready?'

'Just a minute!' Sally had an idea. She beckoned the landlord, that bluff, kindly and no-nonsense Lancastrian. 'Now, Arthur, just in case the boys come in here later, you could drop a gentle hint that we ladies are spending the evening at the arts centre, OK?'

The old man lifted an eyebrow knowingly. 'Happen I'll let them know.'

'Thanks, Arthur. Have a drink on us.' Sally pressed a coin into his hand. 'See you soon.'

The six girls made their way outside. Emma made sure she was last. She couldn't pass Simon without a word. She went to his table, where he sat, his head thrown back with weariness. 'Simon?'

He looked at her, and brought his head back into perpendicular. He smiled a crooked smile. 'Enjoy your evening.'

'But—'

'That's an order. This is how it is—how it will be. Your own words—you have a life to live. You said it, not me. Go and live it, my dear. I have no claim on you, and never did have.'

Yes, she had thrown those words at him—and known at the time that she didn't mean them. But looking at him at that moment made her unable to stir a step from where she was standing. 'I'm being very foolish, but I want to take back what I said,' she told him.

He smiled, and a little light came into his tired blue eyes. 'I won't give up hope, then, Sandy. Maybe spring will come one day. But I wouldn't count on it.'

'Look, friends don't just—stop being friends, do they?'

He looked into her eyes, and the light in his faded in the truth of the moment. 'No, they don't, Sandy. But you were still quite right in reminding me that you're young and have a life to lead. Go along now—don't make me force you!'

Emma tried to joke a little. 'Your guardian angel is giving me trouble—he won't let me move.'

'Oh, my d—' Simon stopped, and bit back the tender words she was longing to hear. He shook his head wearily. 'It's still winter. What can we do?'

'Spring is coming,' she said softly.

He regained his authority and said with mock-sternness, 'But until it does I insist that you go straight to the arts centre and have a great time. You can tell me all about it!'

'But, Simon—'

'I think someone's coming back to look for you.'

Emma sprang away from him, and made a rush for the door, meeting Sally coming in. 'I'm coming, I'm coming!' she called.

## CHAPTER NINE

VERY, very gradually Emma began to realise that she wasn't the only woman in Simon's life. It had been a shock. Parking her car in the very car park where Simon had first berated her for using his space, she noticed his Jaguar, and then before she had time to register the fact she saw a svelte young woman, dressed in a stunning black and white business suit and white boots, getting out of the passenger seat. It was Caroline Brett, from Park Hall Wing. And Caroline seemed to be very happy indeed, for such a cold and frosty morning.

Simon locked his car door, and walked round to take Caroline's elbow, smiling down at her with warmth in his eyes. It was a chilly Friday morning in late January, the trees still glimmered with a coating of frost, and Emma felt the chill very deep down indeed. She huddled over the steering-wheel, unwilling to get out of the car while Simon was there, and hoping against hope that he wouldn't notice her. When she considered that they would be inside the hospital door, she got out, slammed her car door shut, and locked it with unaccustomed firmness.

She told herself that no, of course it didn't matter if Simon Warwick sought solace from his loneliness! Caroline Brett must just have fewer scruples than Emma, that was all. If she wanted to take advantage of a sick woman's husband, then she had every right to do so. But she must have left her conscience in cold storage, that was all Emma could think. Full of righteous indignation, she strode into the ward, and hung up her coat before pinning on her cap. Then she turned, ready to face the day's duties, and to hope and pray that Simon didn't want to stay for coffee after his ward round that morning.

Then she gasped and took a step back. He was already standing in the doorway, in his crisp white coat. 'You took a long time getting out of your car this morning,' he smiled.

'Oh, that was quick, getting your punchline in before mine! You didn't see me. You didn't look round.'

There was still that hint of a smile in his blue eyes. 'I don't have to see you with my eyes, you know, Sandy. I can sense that you're near me without turning round.'

Emma gave a little shiver. Yes, she knew that was true. Why they should have this secret means of communication she didn't know. She said rather acidly, 'I wonder if Caroline has the same advantage?'

'I don't know that. Shall I ask her?'

'You can please yourself, of course.'

He abandoned his flippant tone and said more seriously, 'Actually, Sandy, I wanted to have a word. I have a favour to ask of you.'

'Really?' Emma feigned indifference.

Just then Abina Brown came into the room, and Emma greeted her and hurried off to the ward. If Simon really did want to ask her something, it would just have to wait. They couldn't be seen to be gossiping in private—people might talk.

What about? For a moment Emma felt that all that had happened between them was a dream, that he had never really said all those sweet things to her, called her wise as a fairy. He had even called her beautiful. But Emma compared herself with the gorgeous Caroline, and knew she would never be so glamorous or so sophisticated. She sighed deeply. The patient in the bed beside her said comfortingly, 'Eh, come on now, love. Can't have you letting things get you down. It isn't boyfriend trouble, is it? Not a pretty little thing like you.'

'Boyfriend trouble—me? Not likely, Mrs Stokes. Love 'em and leave 'em, that's what I say.'

'Excuse me, Sister—Charge Nurse MacFarlane on the telephone from Recovery.'

Emma hurried along the ward, hoping that Mac's call wasn't a personal one. She hadn't heard from him for a week, and was hoping that perhaps he was too busy thinking of his next job to have time for her. 'Your pericardectomy patient is ready to come to the ward,' he told her.

'That was quick. Are you sure he's all right?'

Mac sounded ruffled. 'Are you telling me I don't know my job, lass?'

'Sorry. You want us to come and fetch him now? It's Mr Graham, isn't it?'

'As soon as you like, please, Emma. I'll need the bed some time this morning.' He paused, and added, 'It would do my own heart some good if you came for him yourself.'

Emma agreed, good-humouredly. 'I'll see you in a few minutes.'

'Who was that?' Simon had come back with Jerry Green, and they were strolling towards the ward station. 'Sounds like a date to me.'

'A date with Mr Graham,' retorted Emma. 'Your pericardectomy patient. Mac thinks he's OK to be warded.'

'I did leave it to Mac to decide. He's too experienced

a nurse to need me to go and check the patient first. Are you going now?'

'Yes, he needs the bed.'

'I'll walk along with you—I'm going that way,' said Simon. 'Mr Graham has done very well. I'm delighted that I could excise the diseased myocardium without losing too much healthy tissue. The poor chap thought he'd never get better—the heart muscle was so inelastic.'

'He'll be able to live a normal life, then? After all those years as an invalid. How about exercise tolerance?' She felt pleased with herself, being able to have a normal medical conversation with her chief without feeling deprived of that close intimacy they had once shared.

'I'm pretty sure if we mobilise him in gradual stages he can take regular mild exercise. This is where you're very important, Sandy—don't let him get disheartened if his exercise tolerance is slow to return.' Simon suddenly stopped short. 'I say, Sandy, back to that favour I was going to ask—are you doing anything next weekend?'

She was forced to stop in the corridor and face him. 'No.' In this cold grey weather nobody was too anxious to go out, and she had no arrangements made. But surely Simon wasn't going to ask her out? It was against their unwritten agreement.

'Do you mind if I ask you what I started to ask earlier? It's strictly professional, by the way. I'm speaking at a GP symposium on common cardiac surgical problems in Manchester next Saturday, and I want to stress the aftercare aspect. Would you consider coming along with me, and being willing to answer some of the questions on the nursing side of the problems? I thought of you first—you've a lot of experience, and you know I think you're a top-class sister.'

'I——' She was flattered by his offer. 'I suppose I—I can't see why not.' They started to walk along the corridor again, and there was a satisfied smile on Simon Warwick's face. 'How long is this symposium?'

'Saturday and Sunday.' He added casually, 'But we could drive up to Manchester on the Friday night, if you like. Give us a chance to study my notes. It's a long time since I had a friend to share my lonely dinners. Of course, all expenses would be paid.'

'Are you absolutely sure it isn't just a friend you want?'

'Now Sandy, you know me.' His voice lowered into that attractive velvety purr. 'I need a damn good nurse. But I know you'd see through me if I didn't say it—yes, I've wanted to take you out for a slap-up meal for a long time. You deserve it, after all the hard work you put in on my patients. Don't think I haven't noticed. I do want to take you out. But I also want your expertise at the symposium. Is it impossible to combine business with a little innocent pleasure? A single candlelit dinner? Does that sound so very bad?'

'We would—stay in this hotel?'

'Of course—five-star. The sponsor's very generous. And yes, my dear, you will have a separate room—on a different floor, if you don't trust me.'

'I didn't mean——' But they had arrived at Recovery, and Emma rang the bell to ask for admittance. Mac looked through the glass, and did not look overjoyed to see Simon with Emma.

'I've got the porters for you,' he said curtly. His disapproval hovered like an invisible mist round the three of them as they stood together.

'Nice work, Mac.' Simon was appreciative, ignoring the mist. 'You got Mr Graham ready a day earlier than I expected.'

'Aye.' Mac had to grudgingly accept the praise. 'I suppose being comparatively young helped him get over the surgery. Only thirty-seven, he is.'

The porters wheeled the bed into the corridor, while Emma greeted the patient, and checked his notes, and his name-tag. 'I'm glad you're coming back to us, Mr Graham,' she told him.

The man was quietly lying against his pillows, but his face had already lost the blueness round his lips, and his eyes looked alert, not sunken and lifeless as they had before. 'I feel as though I've been in another world for years, and now I'm back to normal. I never thought it would be possible.' He looked up gratefully at Simon. 'They told me at the last hospital that it was a very risky operation, sir. I want to thank you. You ought to be working in London—but for the sake of the people in this neck of the woods I'm damn glad you're here.'

Simon nodded and shook Mr Graham's hand. 'And I'm damn glad you're here, young man! I'm very pleased with your progress. Do you realise that you couldn't say as much as that before the operation without getting breathless?'

'I do realise it, sir. I think that's why Mac wants me out of there—I've been talking too much—singing your praises mostly.'

Emma said, 'Ready to go, Mr Graham? The notes are in order, and I have your medication here.' She turned to accompany the bed, as the porters prepared to push it back to the ward.

Simon said, 'I'll be along to see you later, Mr Graham. You're in good hands.' To Emma he said, 'I won't ask you to decide right away, Sister, about that other matter. But I do hope you don't let such a good opportunity slip away.' And he strode off to renewed thanks from the patient. She noticed Mac looking from one to the other as he returned to the ward.

Emma knew she wanted to accept. The weather had been so miserable recently, and she had been feeling very depressed. Seeing Simon with Caroline Brett hadn't helped—and now he was offering to take her for a weekend in a top hotel, entirely without strings. It would be a refreshing change—like a small holiday. Her life had been nothing but work since the Gareth Price episode, and she was very tempted to say yes to Simon. It did sound very innocent. . .

But promptly at nine that night, the time she knew Mac came off duty, he came sweeping into the common-room, where some of the girls were sitting drinking coffee and watching television. His face was cheerful, and his pleasant Scottish voice casual. 'Emma, I feel like a wee stroll. Come with me for a drink at the inn?'

'Oh—all right. But it's chilly out.'

'All the more reason for a walk! Blow the cobwebs away and get that sluggish circulation going.'

'If you put it like that——' She smiled, and went to get her warmest coat. Mac seemed to be in a good mood, but she remembered the look in his eyes as he had stared at Simon that morning.

They walked along in the crisp starlit evening. 'This was a good idea, Mac. Doesn't the inn look inviting in this cold?' It nestled among the deserted fields that merged into the rolling moorland behind it. Its coloured lights were very welcoming, and the flicker of its fire visible through the leaded windows. She looked up at the ruddy face of the cheerful Pendle witch. 'The old lady's become quite a friend over the past months. I think we all look upon her as an annexe to the hospital!' They sat at a table quite near to the fire, and Mac ordered two lagers, and a plate of pie and chips for himself. Arthur's wife, 'Ma', was famous for her home-made steak pies, and generous portions for hungry nurses.

Mac drank his beer before asking, 'So, how's Mr Graham getting on?'

'He's tired himself out by talking to the others in the ward. Praising Simon to the skies.'

Mac said, 'I canna argue with that. He certainly is a brilliant surgeon. Graham was right—he's been good for the people round here. I agree that all the talent shouldn't be centred in the south. But I wish I kent why he stays. There's precious little here for him.'

'Satisfaction in his job. That's a good reason.' Emma wondered why he was talking about Simon, though she had a good idea where this conversation was leading.

'Nay, everyone says he's henpecked by his wife. She'll no move, so he has to stay put. That's a sign of a weak man, if you ask me.'

Emma said nothing, longing to tell him that the truth was the exact opposite. Simon was one of the strongest men she had ever met—loyal and faithful and principled in the face of enormous privations. But all she said was, 'I don't think he's weak.'

Mac didn't answer, and when she looked up he was staring at her. When her eyes met his, he said, 'And are you going to tell me what he meant when he asked you to consider the "other matter" while you were standing outside my ward?'

'I don't see why not.' Mac was entitled to the truth. She told him, briefly, about the symposium next weekend, as Mac tucked into his steak pie. 'Simon wants me to be there to answer questions on aftercare following surgery—nursing and physio, advice and support, that sort of thing.'

'I see.'

'Oh, don't sound so stuffy, please, Mac. I'd like to go—talk about my job instead of doing it. I know what I'm talking about, and I'd look forward to seeing Manchester again. It would make a nice change.'

Mac stabbed viciously at a chip. 'A nice change for him, you mean? I have to be honest, Emma. It sounds very fishy to me, and I'd think very carefully if I were you. You'd both stay at the same hotel, I suppose?'

So that was where he was leading. Emma said coolly, 'Yes—along with all the other delegates and speakers.'

'And what happens in the evening? A cosy candlelit dinner for two?'

She was glad the atmosphere was dim in the little snug and her blushes didn't show. She wasn't actually lying to him when she answered, because the planned candlelit dinner was on the Friday. 'Actually, Mac, there's a lecture on Saturday evening from nine till ten, followed by a discussion. Simon's in the chair, so I think you're being a little unfair to him. He'll be working very hard.'

'And you won't be?'

She smiled at him. 'It's a long time since I had the chance of some serious window-shopping! When the other lectures are on, I'll take myself round some of the good shops, and probably have my hair cut at a top salon. It will do me the world of good.'

Mac pushed his plate away half finished, and called for more drinks. 'Very plausible. And I canna deny you need a break, Emma. But you ken as well as I do that when a man asks an attractive woman away for the weekend you canna tell me that it's only to answer questions on post-operative procedures!'

Emma looked at him with hurt eyes, unable to keep up her light-hearted answers. He was right to make the point, but she didn't want him to. She was quite aware without being told that there was a risk of being talked about, however innocent Simon's intentions were. She said quietly, 'Mac, do I have to remind you that this is my life, and my decision?'

'I'm sorry. But I feel he's using you, and you're letting him. And what about when everyone hears about it in the hospital?'

She said pointedly, 'They won't unless you tell them.'

'What will you tell your friends if they want you to go out with them?'

'The truth. That I'm going to Manchester to do some shopping.'

'That's a lie for a start.'

'I suppose it is,' she admitted in a small voice. 'But I will be shopping as well.' She sipped her lager. 'Oh, Mac, why isn't life easy?'

'You mean why can't you go right ahead and have an affair with Simon Warwick?' His pain was so obvious, but he had gone too far.

Emma stood up then with blazing eyes. 'That's a terrible thing to say. Simon wouldn't ever do such a thing! He's honourable and good and—oh, strong and brave. I'd trust him to do the right thing wherever we were! You—you shouldn't have said that, Mac. I know him better than you, and I won't have his decent, good name smirched like that!' And she snatched her coat and ran out into the cold night.

Mac caught up with her halfway home. 'Emma, Emma—stop, lass. I didn't mean it.'

She stopped, her breath still coming in gasps and her temper riled. 'I think you did, Mac, and I don't think I can ever think of you the same as I did. You were wrong, and you were cruel.'

He caught her arm and put his arm around her as they started walking again. In a low voice he said against her hair, 'I'm so sincerely sorry. I realise I shouldn't have said that. I just never realised how deep in love you are. I must have been blind. I suppose I'd hoped for you myself. But not any more.' His voice was almost a whisper now. 'I'll be going to Glasgow to work, Emma—there's nothing for me here now. I hoped there might be, but not after tonight.'

She said nothing for a while. She hadn't realised how revealing her outburst was of her inner feelings. After a while she said, 'Yes—well—I'm sorry, Mac. I honestly didn't want this to happen. Things just—happened.'

'It's OK—don't try and explain. I can just see that there's hurt and heartache coming for you if you go on like this, and I've tried to stop it, but you're just going to carry on blindly until you run up against something that could destroy you, Emma. And there's nothing anyone can do about it. Just nothing.'

'Mac, you're a nice person, sincere and good and caring. I've never been the one for you, you know. I do hope you meet someone in Glasgow who's worthy of you.'

'Yes, well, maybe.' He took a deep breath. They were approaching the front gates of the hospital, and the security guard was making sure he knew who they were. Mac's voice changed into his usual cheery self. 'And dinna forget, lassie, that when I leave for Glasgow I expect a send-off worthy of me too! I'll expect a going-away party from your gang that leaves all of us legless. That's an order.'

'You've got it, Mac. At least I can promise you that.'

They waved to the security guard and walked on along the quiet path towards the accommodation blocks. 'Right, then, the party's arranged. Now all I've got to do is make sure I get that job!' He was laughing when he left her, but from her window Emma watched his lanky stride, the dejected set of his head the moment he thought he was out of her sight, and knew something of what he was feeling.

She looked down towards the Pendle Inn. It wasn't all visible from her flat, but there was a glow where its lights lit up the wintry scene. Slowly, thoughtfully she took off her coat. There was something unsettling in the air, and she wasn't sure what it was. The ward came into her mind. Was it the witch? Something was telling her to go to the ward. Something was happening in Orchard—happening to Simon! Pictures of some sort of turmoil, some sort of tragedy made her almost sob. 'Simon, Simon, I'm coming.' She didn't bother with her coat, but, taking only her flat key, she slammed the front door behind her and set off at a run for the hospital building, drawn by the invisible cord that tied her to Simon wherever she was.

The night porter saw her coming, and let her in. 'You're in a hurry, miss.'

'I must go to Orchard,' she panted, as she made for the stairs rather than wait for the lift. Oh, Simon, Simon—the feeling was terrifying, but she knew she must go to him. The doors of the ward were wide open. Night Sister was pacifying the patients. And Mr

# CHAPTER TEN

Mr Graham, to everyone's amazement and delight, continued to make excellent progress. Simon went to see him in Recovery every day, and would come down to the ward to tell the staff. Emma, on duty after four days off, saw him coming along the corridor outside Orchard, and felt suddenly shy at having to come face to face with him, after that dramatic telepathic message that had called her to him. The passion and the emotion of that midnight operation seemed all rather too unreal in the cold light of a normal working day in Orchard Ward.

But she need not have worried. He walked into her office as though it were just an ordinary day. They were alone and, seeing her hesitation, he said at once, 'I was all right once you were with me. I knew I could save him, but I needed that little bit of extra confidence and encouragement. I don't often admit that I'm not God Almighty in that theatre, and I didn't say anything to anyone else about you. I knew you'd come. When you came——' He spoke in a low voice, but there was no embarrassment in admitting it to her. 'With you, I'm complete, you know.'

That was how she felt too. But she felt unable to say anything, feeling, as she always did these days, the pale form of his fragile wife hovering between them. Simon read her thoughts, and almost touched her arm in a spontaneous gesture of solidarity and understanding. But his common sense prevailed, and he turned away, to get on with his usual ward round. Someone had a bowl of primulas at the bedside, and he said with more than usual cheerfulness, 'Spring's almost here, then!'

Spring. It had been a magic word for Emma, a message of hope—but not now. She couldn't see what difference the changing of the seasons could possibly mean to her. She would still love Simon, and Simon would still be totally and irrevocably married.

On his way from the ward, after a brief and almost silent ward round, he paused at the office, where Emma was putting the notes away and entering his latest remarks in them. 'Oh, Sister—I'll be including Mr Graham's case in my lecture on Saturday.'

She looked up with a sudden smile. Without thinking, she said, 'Your latest success? I should think so too. And—I would like to be included in the trip, if the offer still stands.'

'It stands.' She heard suppressed delight in his voice.

'And—my separate room stands too, I hope?' She looked down shyly at her notes.

'On my honour.'

Emma said quietly, 'That's enough for me.'

When he didn't reply she looked up again from her work. There was a light in the blue eyes that reminded her of spring. He said softly, 'That's the nicest thing anyone has ever said to me.'

It was difficult not to go on talking to him, share the delight and joy of their mutual success. But Emma kept her head down, and did not lift it until she knew he had left the room. After he had gone, Sally Briggs poked her head round the door. 'Are you busy, Em?'

'Not terribly. Did you want something?'

'I just wanted to tell you something that maybe you hadn't noticed.'

'I notice everything around here!' Emma pretended to scold her.

'Maybe not that Mr Warwick hasn't shouted at anyone for at least a month. Did you know that?'

Emma looked carefully at Sally, but there didn't seem to be an ulterior motive in what she said. She was just expressing something she had noticed for herself. Emma smiled, and said, 'I must say I hadn't realised. . .'

'Em, they're saying that you've tamed him, you know. It only happened after you came, and you started standing up to him in your own quiet but firm way.'

Emma sat up straight. This was it. The gossip was starting. Of course, after her dramatic midnight entrance into the operating theatre there was hardly any point in denying her special relationship with Simon. But for his sake, and Liz's sake, she didn't admit anything. 'Yes, maybe you're right. I'm surprised nobody had told him to his face before that his temper caused disruption on the ward.'

Sally admitted it, and again it didn't sound as though she was prying into Emma's private life. 'We just accepted that Mr Warwick was bad-tempered,' she shrugged. 'We blamed his wife, forcing him to stay where she worked, instead of giving him the chance of moving to a bigger hospital. But it can't be that, if he's getting better and he's still married.' And Emma allowed her to chatter on, knowing that the more Sally talked, the less Emma needed to say.

Then Sally said, 'How about a night on the town on Saturday? The nights are getting lighter, and I'm getting itchy feet.'

Not this weekend, this very special weekend. . . 'I'm—thinking of going home on Friday, actually, Sally,' Emma told her. 'I haven't given Mum much of my time recently.' It was a lie, but only a white one to save Simon's reputation—and her own. 'Let's make it the following week, shall we?'

'OK. But I'm going to drag that hunky Scotsman of yours out even if you're not there!'

'Good! I'm glad! He needs a bit of entertainment.' Poor Mac. She hadn't been in touch with him since his admission of his own affection for her and his determination to leave Forrestall. It would be nice if Sally persuaded him to join the group on Saturday.

That evening Emma stepped out of the shower, her thoughts a jumble of pity for Mac, admiration and gratitude to Sally for being such a staunch friend and avoiding topics she knew would embarrass Emma, and of course adoration and worship of Simon, the truest husband and most honourable any wife could ever have. She enveloped herself in a towelling robe, just as her telephone rang. 'Sandy?'

Only one man used that name. 'Yes, Simon.' Her heart beat faster, even though she trusted his integrity. It was almost as though they were lovers, the way her evening was brightened by just one word from him. Yet this weekend was a business trip with a colleague, nothing more. . .

'I thought I'd better make arrangements with you by phone. You haven't changed your mind about the weekend? I didn't want to talk in front of the staff. You never know in the ward who might overhear scraps of conversation.'

'I know. It's happened. Mac heard you asking me about this weekend when we were all outside Recovery with Mr Graham.'

She heard Simon breathe in deeply. 'So he knows?'

'He promised to say nothing.'

'Let's hope nothing slips out—for your sake more than mine. Sandy, I think it best if you take your car to the inn after work on Friday. Put your weekend bag in the boot. I'll meet you in the inn car park at about six, we'll leave your car there, and we'll drive down from there in mine.'

He had obviously worked it all out for the best. 'OK. That sounds fine—if a little furtive.'

'You don't mind, do you? I hate to put you through this, but it seems wisest. We're doing nothing wrong, my dear, but it does make sense to keep hospital gossip to a minimum.'

'It's very sensible, and I'll do that. There's no need to mention it in the ward.'

'Good. Sandy—I——' He stopped. Was he going to say he loved her? It was hard to tell. She sensed the words hanging in the air. Yet, after all, she wasn't the only female he gave lifts to. The sight of Caroline Brett in his car had given her quite a jolt. She must still keep up her defences, and not allow any opportunity for them to be alone together if possible.

Next morning when Simon came in to work he was as good as his word. He talked to Jerry Green about the cases he was going to describe at the symposium, and even asked Emma to get out the relevant notes for him to take home and read up. All he said to Emma was, 'It's important for anyone who's going to speak in front of a hundred or so people to have the facts at their fingertips.'

'Of course. I realise that. I'll have them ready for you by this evening.' Emma knew that he wanted her to read them up too, and have their treatment and medication written down in case he needed to refer to it. She made a careful list of the cases. A couple of patients were from before Emma had come to Forrestall, and she had to ask Abina Brown if the notes were full enough, and correct in every detail.

On Friday, Simon hardly spoke to Emma in the ward. It added to her excitement, which had started with the first rays of a pale February sunshine lighting up the traces of snow that still lay in the hollows of the moors. She had packed a change of underclothes, and two decent dresses. At the last minute she stuck in her jeans. She would travel in her one and only good suit, a Prince of Wales check that by its very smartness emphasised the elfin prettiness of the wearer. As she tucked the bag into the boot of her car in the quietness of very early morning, she couldn't believe that in less than twelve hours she would be sitting beside Simon, and they would be going away for a totally honourable and businesslike weekend. Even that was more than she could ever have hoped, in the history of their strange and unconventional relationship.

Jerry had wished Simon well. 'Do you know any of the other lecturers on this course?'

'I know the transplant team from Wythenshawe—they'll be the star attraction. And of course I know the prof from Manchester University. We studied together.'

Emma wondered if he felt very much out of the mainstream of surgery, stuck out in the Lancashire moors. But he had been here so long that he was probably immune to feelings of regret. Jerry Green voiced something of what Emma was thinking. 'But you are the big chief here, sir—with a string of successes that must be a lot longer than theirs.'

'Yes, Jerry, I'll be telling them some of the more challenging cases I've had. One thing about being out here is that I've had to tackle a wider variety of heart conditions than the big boys ever get to. I'm certainly not sorry I took on Forrestall—not sorry at all.'

Dressed in her best suit after work, Emma walked down the avenue of sycamores, where one or two buds were just beginning to show a hint of new fresh green. She noticed them, but was a lot more concerned at that moment about not being seen by anyone she knew. She reached the car park and slipped quickly into the driving seat, looking neither to right nor left until she was safely strapped in and had switched the engine on. Her heart thudded with excitement, and her palms sweated and had to be wiped with her best embroidered handkerchief.

She drove to the hospital gates. There was a lone figure making his way across the grass to the dining-rooms, and she knew it was Mac. Whether he was there on purpose she couldn't know. But she knew he would recognise her car, even though she increased her speed, and didn't look round. In the mirror, she saw that he had stopped and was looking after her. She lifted one hand from the wheel and waved briefly, sensing his disapproval even at that distance.

The Pendle Inn was quiet, the evening rush not yet begun, and the car park almost empty. Emma drove right to the back behind the inn, and hoped none of her friends would spot the car over the weekend and recognise it as hers. There she sat, her pulses racing, wondering if he really would come, for about five minutes, until Simon's green Jaguar nosed its way round the corner and stopped. He jumped out with a smile. He was obviously not disconcerted by this secret tryst. 'Well done, Sandy. Give me your bag. I say, you do look great. Thanks for coming, by the way. It means a lot to me.' He took her hand for a moment and drew her fractionally nearer to him. He wasn't to know her frustration at being so close to that tweedy jacket, to smell the maleness of him yet be unable to touch him as she yearned to do. 'But of course you know that.' He had helped her into the luxurious passenger seat and locked her bag in his boot while he was talking. Now he came round and sat beside her. 'Nervous?'

Emma smiled back, determined not to admit it. 'Certainly not.'

'Still sure you really want to come?'

'Of course! I've got my hair appointment booked for ten in the morning in King Street.'

Simon laughed aloud. 'Well done, Sandy. Though from where I'm sitting your hair looks pretty enough without the attentions of King Street!' They were soon purring along the main road from Forrestall to Manchester, and, glancing at his Rolex, Simon confirmed that they would be there just in time for dinner. He put on a tape—Beethoven's First Piano Concerto—and for a while they said nothing, busy with their own thoughts.

Finally Emma said, 'Your temper's improved, so they tell me.'

'Really? You see what can be done when you get a really cross sister on the ward.'

'Is it really anything to do with me?'

'I hadn't even thought about it. But yes—you were the first to lecture me instead of taking it sitting down. That's true.' And after a while he went on, 'And maybe meeting you made me a happier man.'

'It made a difference to me too.'

'It gave you more hassle, I recognise that.'

'That's right. You're a very perceptive person.'

He smiled at her before looking back at the road. 'I'll look forward to arguing about my good and bad points later this evening. Just now, would you be very kind and look out for signs to the university? There's been a lot of new building since I was here last, and I'd lose face if we got lost.'

'What hotel do I look out for?' asked Emma.

'The Piccadilly, but I can find that easily once we make the right turn into Oxford Road. We pass the medical school—the largest in Europe, by the way—then the university and the poly, on the left, the BBC on the right, followed by the Palace theatre, and we're almost there.'

'As long as you can point me in the direction of King Street——'

'No problem. I'll take you there before I start in the morning.'

They left the car at the imposing entrance to the high modern block that was the Piccadilly hotel. Simon left the engine running, and a hotel porter took their bags from the boot before driving the car off to park. They were greeted politely by the immaculate blonde behind the desk. 'If you'll just register, Dr Warwick.' And she was surprised when Emma took the pen and signed her own name underneath Simon's. She assumed I was his fancy woman, thought Emma, slightly annoyed. But on the other hand it was hard not to be flattered to have the attention of the lean and aggressively handsome Simon, his face taut with tiredness, but his eyes clear and intelligent, his bearing naturally aristocratic. Any woman would be proud to be with a man like Simon. She noticed for the first time that there were a few silver hairs in the black, just over his ears, and wondered how it must feel to live almost a lifetime with a woman who could never be a wife, yet who must always be treated with respect and devotion.

She said quietly, as they went up in a silent lift to the fifth floor, 'I think that woman at the desk expected you to write Mr and Mrs Smith.'

Simon roared with laughter. 'Oh, Sandy, didn't I promise?'

'You did. I don't mind really.'

'My dear, it's done openly now. There's no need to pretend.' He opened a door with one of the keys he had been given. 'This is your room. I'm next door.'

Her bag was already on the side-shelf. There was a single rose in a crystal vase on the dressing-table, and on the small table in the window was a silver pail containing a bottle of champagne, with two glasses, a bowl of savouries and two snow-white napkins. Emma stared, then turned to go to the door and call Simon. But his voice came from just beside her. 'Like it?'

When she looked up, she realised that he had appeared through an adjoining door, to which he held the key. He smiled broadly. 'Don't worry, Emma, you won't need this. I'm a man of my word. I swear I didn't know there was an interconnecting door.' And he laid the key on her dressing-table. 'You're totally in charge of that, Sandy. Now, after we've had a much needed drink, I'll leave you to shower and change, and we'll go down to the dining-room for the best meal they can offer us.'

She said, 'You must think me a small-town kid, to let all this luxury overwhelm me like this.'

His voice was deep and serious as he stood in front of her and held her gently by the arms. 'No, Emma. How can you call yourself that? To be honest, I can't tell you how much I think of you. Any man would be proud to be seen with you, you know. You have principles, you have kindness and you have taste. It's easy to have principles when you're ninety-two and ugly with it, but to have a devastatingly pretty girl like you—someone who could have any man she chose—well, it's a privilege to be able to call you my friend.' There was no echo of condescension in his comments. He was merely telling her the truth, and she reddened at his sincerity.

She asked him something she had wanted to ask for days. 'Does—Caroline—have principles?'

She couldn't see him smiling, because his back was towards her as he opened the champagne, but she heard the smile in his voice. 'You know, I wondered when her name would come up. You watched her that day I gave her a lift, didn't you, Sandy? I do believe you were a tiny bit jealous.'

Emma didn't admit it. 'What sort of girl is she?'

'I hardly know her.' He turned round, popped the cork with a satisfying plop, and poured the resultant foaming liquid into the two glasses. Emma had to express her astonishment. She joked, 'For someone who lives as quietly as you do, that was done with remarkable skill.'

Simon handed her a glass. His face was innocent, and she was glad to see the lines of tiredness were smoothing out. He said, 'Any manual dexterity is entirely due to a long and blameless career in cardiac surgery, my dear. It keeps the fingers supple! Now let's drink to—the success of—the symposium.'

Emma said, just as innocently. 'That's why we're here. To the symposium.' She touched the lip of her glass against his, before realising she was very thirsty, and sipping the excellent champagne with a sense of pure luxury.

He sat down at the little table and drew out the programme for the weekend. Loosening his tie, he said, 'Now, let's make sure we know exactly where we'll both be, and when we have to meet.'

'And how to find Kendal Milnes. And King Street.' She sat down opposite him.

He refilled their glasses. 'Not bad champagne, is it? I hope you like the widow.'

She looked at the label. Veuve Clicquot. 'The widow Clicquot. There must be a history behind that label.'

'There must be. Do you like it?'

'Oh, yes—very much. But I don't think I should have any more.'

'You'll be OK, little wise woman. But I'll leave you now to have your shower and get dressed. I'll come back for you at—' He consulted his Rolex. 'How long does it take a woman to get ready?'

She looked up at him, suddenly full of pity that a man who had been married for so long, who had fulfilled the harrowing terms of his marriage contract to the letter, had never enjoyed the little things, had never known what it was like to live a normal life with a loving wife. She found there was a lump in her throat as she said, 'Not long. Just knock when you're ready, Simon.'

He opened the connecting door. 'You're in charge of the key, Sandy.' And, taking his glass of champagne with him, he went through to his own room and closed the door between them.

She felt quite heady with the champagne, but not tipsy, just exhilarated and happy. She went over some of his compliments to her that evening. He thought her very pretty, very wise, and a woman of principles. . . She felt a shiver go through her body at the thought of him changing in the very next room, at the idea that they could go to each other at any time—unless she locked that door. Very deliberately she pushed her glass against the connecting doorkey, so that it fell, almost accidentally, from the dressing-table into the waste-paper basket. 'There go my principles, Simon,' she whispered. 'Now you're going to need enough for both of us.'

When he did call for her, he didn't even try the connecting door, but knocked at her own door. Emma answered it, dressed in her favourite fitted dress of soft crimson angora, with a wide suede belt of the same colour, and tiny rubies in her ears. He stood, dark hair waving back, blue eyes very blue and very appreciative, in a dark grey suit, white shirt and university tie. His shoes reflected the lights in the corridor. After a moment, he said in a rather husky voice, 'I think I'd better ask to change my room. I know I won't be able to resist you when you look like that.'

She sensed again that sweet languor that came when they were alone together, the feeling of union and total joy and completeness. In a low voice, she said, 'No—please don't.'

'You're accepting responsibility, then? For—for——' He took her hand and drew her towards him, giving her shoulders a squeeze and not taking his arm away.

'I'm hungry, Simon.' She thought it best that they didn't put their secret desires into words. It would be harder to deny them in the cold light of day.

In the lavish dining-room, among crowds of well-dressed and glittering couples, they were shown a table for two in a subtly lit alcove. A single red candle flickered on the table between them, and a waiter welcomed them with deference. He drew out Emma's chair and seated her with her napkin unfolded with a flourish and draped on her lap. '*Madame* would care for a drink before dinner?'

*Madame* wouldn't, but didn't want to appear unsophisticated. 'Yes, please.'

'Sir?'

Simon spoke for both of them. 'We'll have our usual, shall we, darling?' She nodded, terribly grateful that he had taken charge. He ordered iced mineral water, and within moments of two blessedly cool glasses appearing a bottle of mineral water was placed discreetly at Simon's elbow. 'I hope you don't mind, Sandy, but we both need to have a clear head in the morning,' he explained.

'Thank goodness. I didn't have a clue what to ask for. I must say I'm more in the jeans and hamburger set. I don't think I've ever dined in such state.'

He ordered again for them—melon, grilled halibut with tiny new potatoes and fresh vegetables, a sorbet and a sliver of Stilton cheese. They chatted easily—of the day to come, of the hospital, of individual cases which they had both had a part in curing. 'We'd better have tea rather than coffee,' Simon decided. 'You need some beauty sleep.'

Emma wouldn't have dreamt of asking for tea, but she was very grateful when it came, fresh and strong. The candle flickered and danced between them. Simon said, 'Since that first night when we sat at the corner table in the Pendle, I've wanted to see you like this, you know. If I'd dared, I'd have asked you out for dinner, and given myself just a little bit of pleasure before I told you the truth about my pathetic little life. But I'm glad I didn't. It's better this way, with you knowing all about me, and still accepting my invitation. My conscience is clear. I hope it will be tomorrow.'

'You look different by candlelight, you know. Your eyes are alive and happy. Do I look different? More than a hundred years old?' she teased.

For the first time that evening he reached across and touched her hand. 'You look—everything I've ever dreamed of, Sandy. Everything.'

# CHAPTER ELEVEN

THE mist swirled over the moors, and the ewes called in the early morning around Forrestall, answered by the high anxious bleating of their tiny, new white lambs. But in the centre of Manchester, thirty miles away, Emma stirred and opened her eyes, wondering for a moment where she was, why the bed was so incredibly comfortable, and why she was feeling just a little depressed.

There was a knock on the door. She sat up and looked. Which door was it? But the connecting door opened and Simon came in, his hair ruffled, unshaven and wearing only pyjama trousers, with a tray in his hands. 'Your morning call, *madame*.' He came to the bed, bent and kissed her lips rather longer than was strictly brotherly, and set the tray on the bedside table. 'Good morning, Sandy. You do like tea in bed?'

'I've never had it. But I could get used to it.'

'Good. I'm sorry to disturb you, but I need to make an early start. I want to go over my papers, and the symposium starts at nine. I'll take a taxi over, and if you like I'll drop you in St Ann's Square first.'

'Thank you.' Emma knew why she was depressed. Simon had been just a little bit too proper. True, he had showered her with compliments, and had even kissed her a couple of times as he said goodnight. But she had been mentally prepared for warding him off, and it had been disappointing to have nothing to ward off. At her bedroom door, he had cupped her cheek in one hand

and whispered, 'Night, Sandy.' She couldn't argue with that. It was only the correct way for a married man to behave.

'Lunch at the Ramada—buffet thing,' he told her. 'Want to join me there, or meet me outside? Our lecture starts at three—old Parker's doing an update on the new anti-rejection drugs they use at Wythenshawe first.'

'I think we ought to lunch there. It would look rather obvious if I came in halfway through.'

'Right. I hope you enjoy your morning.' He kissed her on the forehead. 'Drink your tea. I'll knock on the door when I'm dressed, to go down for breakfast.'

Her depression soon lifted when she lost herself in the splendours of shopping. Boutiques, and salons, chain stores and exclusive designer clothes—Emma wandered like a child in a sweetshop until it was time for her hair appointment. Then she was pampered by one of the top stylists, a slim young man called Nigel, given coffee and biscuits, and restyled with a trendy modern hairdo. Her purse the lighter for thirty pounds—her mother would have a fit if she knew!—Emma decided she must have a trendy new outfit to go with it. She went back to the boutiques, and bought herself some high boots, leggings and a huge coloured designer sweater with a roll collar that was snugger than her coat.

She had to take her shopping back to the hotel. Then, wearing her suit, and feeling very much the career woman, she took the lift down and asked the doorman to hail a cab for her. Carrying her briefcase, she said, 'The Ramada, please.'

She wasn't nervous at meeting the Professor and the consultants—having worked among their like all her life, she knew well that, however smartly they dressed, and however plummy some of their accents were, they were all very human, with troubles and worries like the rest of humanity. She pushed open the door of the dining-room, where groups of people stood about chatting earnestly, with plates of quiche and salad in one hand and glasses of white wine in the other. Several heads turned at her entrance, and she noticed a rustle of interest among the men. She saw Simon standing with a vivacious woman at the bar. The woman was laughing loudly, and Emma paused before butting in. But by that time Simon had noticed her too, and his face lit up. He quickly excused himself, and came towards her with outstretched hands. 'Sandy, my little Sandy, what have you done to yourself? You look magnificent.'

'Only had a haircut—oh, and I thought I'd better put on a bit of make-up to go with it. Wait till you see what I bought!'

Simon glanced around, and most of the interested eyes returned to their quiche at his proprietorial stance. 'Whatever you paid for that hair, it was worth it. You look like a film star.'

'You mean a haircut can make such a difference?'

'You had the looks before, but—Sandy, Sandy, what a knockout you are today. I thought you suited the casual look, but I love this glossy modern woman you've turned into. And what on earth is that stuff you've got round your eyes? They look twice the size they were this morning. I'm very proud to be with you. Now, what can I get you to eat?'

'It looks as though it's quiche, quiche or quiche.'

'Something like that.'

'Well, just a little, please.'

'Don't blame you. We'll make up for it tonight, eh?'

They settled into their seats while the chairman called the meeting to order and introduced the first speaker of the afternoon. Emma listened to what he had to say, but didn't take notes. She was hardly likely to work with heart transplant patients, though it was fascinating to hear what progress had been made since that first fateful operation in South Africa that was condemned by so many of the surgical fraternity.

When Simon took the rostrum, she watched him with anxious eyes. Would he betray anything of the country boy, working out in 'the sticks' as compared with these high-fliers on the panel? But she need not have worried. He spoke as the equal of every man and woman in that room, and he was right to do so. As he began to list the various operations he had been able to do because he was the only surgeon in the area, some people began to look quite envious. When he described Mr Graham's cardiopathology, there were expressions of surprise that he had even tackled it, instead of putting him on the list for transplant. 'Of course,' he went on, 'this patient was only in the ward for—four days, wasn't it, Sister Sandiford?'

Emma nodded. Simon smiled, as the audience waited for him to confess that Mr Graham had died. 'I had to get him back to Theatre at midnight. His BP was barely there. I knew there was no time to do anything but open up the chest again.' People sat up in their seats. 'It took five hours to find all the bleeding sources.' He paused. 'But it proved to be well worth doing. When does Mr Graham go home, Sister Sandiford?'

'On Monday.' Emma's voice was clear.

Simon received a generous ovation when he stood down. The chairman announced that he would take questions, and Simon beckoned Emma to come and sit beside him. She was very conscious of the fact that from the raised dais her legs were even more visible, and she tried not to be self-conscious, aware that her legs were nothing to be ashamed of. Simon answered the questions on individual cases, explaining that he had asked Emma to be with him because as they were part of a very small surgical team it was vital that the post-operative nursing and physiotherapy be of the highest quality, and that the medication was reviewed if necessary more than once a day. They discussed their cases, Emma relieved that she had memorised all the case-notes, and didn't need to refer to the notes she had brought in her briefcase.

Afterwards Simon thanked her. 'Not only for being sensible and intelligent when you answered the questions, but also for making me proud to be with the best-looking woman in the room.'

'I'm so glad I came, Simon. I was the proud one, to be associated with all you've done. When I came to Forrestall I had no idea I was to meet the famous S. T. Warwick. Now I know just how eminent you really are.'

Simon tried to shrug off her praise, but he was clearly flattered by her open admiration. The platform party milled around them. 'I hope you can come back for the discussion this evening,' the Professor said to them both.

Emma waited for Simon to reply on her behalf, and he accepted politely. 'Of course. Time for a good old chinwag, David. It's been a long time.'

The rest of the audience were drifting towards the dining-room for cups of tea. There was a GP forum after tea and then delegates made for the bars. Several men came over to speak to Emma, including one of the transplant team. Simon found himself on the outside of an admiring group, and she saw that he wasn't enjoying it very much, especially when the transplant man asked her if she had ever thought of working in Wythenshawe.

He took her hand firmly as soon as he got the chance. 'Terribly sorry, everyone, but we have an appointment——' He dragged her bodily from the hall, and out into the chill of early evening. Emma gasped at the cold, at the number of cars and buses, and the sheer numbers of people. 'Town is rather fun sometimes,' she said. 'All bustle and excitement.'

'You were having just a little bit too much fun for me.'

'Simon—you're having one of your moods again. I thought I'd cured you of that.'

'Not when the entire college of GPs is following you with their tongues hanging out,' he laughed. He managed to wave down a taxi. 'We're not going back to that discussion, and that's for sure.'

'We're not?'

'Don't tell me you want to.'

'I think you have an important part to play in a discussion about cardiac surgery. I don't, though. Tell you what—I'll meet you after the discussion.'

'Where will you be?' he asked.

'I thought I'd go to the theatre. The Royal Exchange.'

'And where shall we have dinner, then?'

They had reached the Piccadilly, and went up to their rooms in silence. Emma opened her door. 'Do come in, Simon—I want to show you what I bought!'

He looked on as she spilled out her purchases on the bed. 'What do you think?' she queried.

'I think I'm being left out. You're sending me off to the discussion, while you dress up and go out on the town!'

'Well, let's do it now, then!'

'Do what?'

'Dress up and go out on the town. You've brought some jeans, haven't you?'

'Yes.'

'Right. Jeans and sweater, while I put this lot on. Then we'll walk along the streets, and window-shop, and have a drink at some naughty little club, and have dinner at McDonald's.'

Simon laughed aloud with sheer pleasure. 'You're a genius. Oh, Sandy, am I glad I brought you! I'll be five minutes.'

'You're not having a shower?'

'Yes. I'll still be five minutes.' He bent and kissed her cheek, before opening the connecting door. 'I say, where's the key?'

'I've no idea,' said Emma innocently. He gave her a hard stare, and then smiled knowingly as he saw it glinting in the waste basket, before disappearing into his own room.

They walked along the pavements, round the Arndale Centre and into St Ann's Square, holding hands like happy children. There were some clowns there, and a busker with a little monkey entertaining the rush-hour crowds. They were jostled and pushed in the mêlée, but people were usually well-mannered, and apologised if they stood on a foot. A photographer snapped them before they realised it, and thrust a card into Simon's hand. 'Ready for you in two hours, squire.'

They went into the Royal Exchange brasserie for a drink. It was almost as crowded in there, but they found a little table, and sat close together, laughing and discussing whether they should actually go and get the photograph, and whether Simon really ought to go to the discussion later that evening.

They decided that they had to have that photograph,

and trailed round the side-streets looking for the address on the photographer's card. Two copies of the picture were ready for them, and outside they stood for a long time studying them.

'We look like honeymooners,' said Simon slowly. The laughing faces, the closeness, the way they were looking at each other. . . It was an intimate glimpse into their subconscious, and Simon put his photograph into his wallet. 'Look after it, Sandy.' She nodded, and looked at it again before putting it back in its envelope and into her shoulder-bag. It pained her a little, seeing them as they could have been, if there hadn't been any Liz between them, simple and innocent in her affliction.

She watched him lovingly, very aware that he had never had this kind of innocent fun for many years, and glad that she was privileged to see Simon really enjoy himself for one night of his life. They began to laugh again in McDonald's. They ate cheeseburgers and apple pie, drank chocolate milk shakes, and wondered what all their colleagues at Forrestall were doing at that moment. If they could see Simon and Emma now, they would hardly believe what they saw, a carefree couple very comfortable together, and out to have as much fun as they could. Emma said, 'The Saturday night feeling. It's fun isn't it?'

Simon agreed, 'It can be, I know. But usually I'd be at home, feeding Liz.'

Emma waited, but he didn't go on. She said, urging him to open up to her at last, knowing that tonight was the best time, while they were relaxed and happy, 'Tell me about it, Simon. You must have had some good times before she——'

He looked at her, and reached out to stroke her new-look glossy hair. 'Oh, Sandy, Sandy, if only you knew——'

'Tell me.'

'What?'

'Why not? Tell me. I'm your friend, aren't I?'

He nodded, and looked down, uncertain suddenly, now that the time had come. He started hesitantly, as he dredged up memories that he didn't really want to recall. 'We'd been married four months. It went wrong on honeymoon, when I found out she'd only pretended to be pregnant. When she fell ill, I was on the point of telling her that I knew I'd made a mistake, and asking for a divorce.' He stopped, choked with memories, and then went on slowly, 'When I saw what she was like after the illness, I thought she was pretending—doing it to make me feel guilty. I soon found out that her mind had gone forever.'

'But why did things go wrong so quickly?'

His voice had never been bitter before, but now it was. His eyes were miserable. 'I genuinely believed her when she said she was pregnant, and I meant to make a go of it. We seemed to get on well, and she never showed her selfish side when we were going out together. I tried hard to be understanding, but it was no good. It wasn't Liz's fault really—I realised later that her mother had put her up to it because she thought it was a good thing to do, to marry a doctor. Brainwashed, she was, by that mother of hers—the mother who never comes near us now.'

Emma's mouth had fallen open. She murmured, 'Simon, oh, Simon.'

'It wasn't Liz's fault, you see. She was too dumb to think up an idea like that for herself, and too dumb to understand that she didn't really love me—just the idea of being a doctor's wife. She worked—in her mother's business as some sort of secretary. I—thought I loved her. She was beautiful once, you know. Her hair was thick and luxurious, a lovely shade of chestnut. Sandy, I'd stood before God and made those promises about sickness and health, richer and poorer. . . I knew I had to take care of her. She has no one else, and I couldn't let her go into a mental hospital forever. I hoped her mother would help me, but she sold the business and went to live in Spain. She didn't tell me where. . .'

Emma put her hand gently on Simon's. 'Does anyone else know this?'

'Bill Kenyon knows about her mother. I—didn't tell him about—wanting a divorce. It—suddenly became irrelevant.'

She felt drained of feeling. To help him get over the shock of having to confess all that he had kept hidden for so long she changed the subject, saying gently, 'How about another milk shake?'

He smiled gratefully. 'Chocolate or strawberry?'

Later they walked back to the hotel in silence. The discussion had started at the symposium, but neither of them mentioned it. Simon's story lay like a lead weight wrapped round both of them, taking the spring from their step and the light from their eyes. As they rounded a corner into Deansgate, Simon put his arm round Emma's shoulders, and they walked linked together. 'It's a lovely sweater, Sandy. Must have cost you a bomb.'

'A bomb and a half, actually.'

'But you don't regret it?'

'I don't regret anything.'

Simon swore under his breath. 'You're trying to be cheerful, my dear, and you can't be—I can tell. I shouldn't have told you. I shouldn't put anyone who likes me through the hell I've been through. And I don't want you pitying me either. I chose this life, you know, and I'll stick by it.'

'Good for you.'

He stopped in the busy street, both of them ignoring the people passing by them. He took her face in both his hands and kissed the tip of her nose. 'And Sandy—thank you for one of the nicest nights of my life. It's been wonderful, being real—living a real life, having fun. . .' They sat on a bench in Piccadilly Gardens and blew at their hands to keep warm. There were fewer people there, and they could hear themselves talk. 'If things were different, Sandy, would you marry me?'

She said quietly, 'I think you know the answer to that one.'

He sighed deeply. 'Well, listen to me, Sandy. I'm going to be very serious now. I owe it to you, now that you know all about me. You're not to wait for moonshine, for a spring that may never come. I want you, starting the minute we get back to Forrestall, to live your life as though you'd never met me, understand? Go out a lot. Spring is coming, and you're young enough to enjoy it. Every time I see you outside the hospital, I want it to be with a different bloke. For God's sake, Sandy, make the most of every minute while you're young.'

She didn't answer. He knew her well enough to realise that what he was suggesting wasn't possible. Not right away anyway. Not after telling her that she was his other half, that without her he wasn't complete. He said, 'Want to go back?'

'All right.'

'Would you—link your arm through mine? I've

always wondered what it would feel like, walking along with a woman you can be proud of, a woman the fellows turn their heads to get a good look at.'

Emma put her hand in the crook of his elbow, and he put his other hand over hers and smiled down at her as they started to walk back to the hotel. She said, 'I'm not sure if I ought to stay in Orchard Ward when we get back.'

'I know how you feel. I suppose I didn't want to tell you all this for fear of losing you. But—well, the other girls in Orchard are good. You've trained them well, dear. I'm sorry I shouted at them so much. They were only doing their job. I can work with them quite well. The only snag is they don't read my mind as you've always done.'

She nodded, knowing it was true. Still looking at the pavement as they walked, she said, 'I might apply to—Glasgow.'

'Why Glasgow?'

'There's a job going at the Royal Southern—a good job. Mac wrote to their personnel department for a list of vacancies. And my mother is much better able to cope now.'

After a while he said, 'Tell me when you apply. I'll give you a reference that'll get you the job right away.'

She said, 'You aren't saying goodbye, are you? You'll write to me sometimes?'

'I'll promise to send you a Christmas card.'

'They have more fun at Hogmanay in Glasgow. Singing and dancing and piping and first-footing. . .'

'You've been talking to Mac a lot.'

'Yes.'

They walked up the staircase, wanting to stay with their arms linked as long as possible. Up the grand and deserted staircase they went, nearer and nearer on the thick carpet, their feet making no noise, to the moment when they would have to separate. At the door, she said, 'Come and have coffee.'

'No, thank you, Sandy. You've had enough of me and my troubles for the time being. Goodnight, my sweet Sandy. I'll see you at breakfast.'

She lost herself in the warmth of his sweater, hugging him tightly for a moment. Then she pulled away, her eyes unseeing, fumbled for her key, and let herself into her room. She closed the door behind her, and walked over to sit on the bed, tears dripping down her cheeks.

After a while she realised she was hot, and pulled the glorious new sweater off. She was wearing a T-shirt underneath. She slowly pulled the elegant boots off, then the leggings, and lay on the bed in briefs and T-shirt, waiting for sleep that wouldn't come.

There was a little tap at the connecting door. Emma had put the light out, and only the street-lights illumined the room. 'Yes?'

Simon stood outlined in the doorway, wearing only briefs. 'If you wanted to go back to Forrestall tonight, I don't mind driving you. You must wish you hadn't come.'

She sat up against the pillows and held out a hand mutely to him. He sat on the edge of the bed, and she held his hand in both hers. 'I don't know what I feel. Only that——' How could she tell him she wanted to be near him, when they had just decided to part? She said, 'I threw the key in the waste-paper basket.'

'I know. Why would you do that?'

'Maybe I couldn't help myself. What made me come to the inn that first time? What made me come to the theatre that night you operated on Mr Graham?'

'What made me come to you now?' He lay beside her on the bed, and pulled her into his arms. His chest was warm, and she felt the little black hairs on it as she nuzzled against him. He rolled her gently on to her back and pulled up the T-shirt so that he could kiss her breasts. Gently he took the shirt and her briefs from her, and she helped him get rid of his briefs. It was warm in that luxury bedroom, so warm that they didn't need to go inside the bed, and they could see the full length of each other's body by the light from the street-lamp, a neon sign beneath their floor flashing off and on as their lips came together in a kiss that neither of them could stop. 'Is it wrong, Sandy? I did make you a promise. Something about my honour——'

Her breathing was erratic now, and she could only stop his murmured questions with a lingering kiss. 'I don't know anything any more.'

'I'll never stop loving you, you know. But you have to obey me and forget about me. Is that clear?' He was whispering, as he covered her body with kisses, every inch that he could reach, pushing her legs apart to reach even further with delicate feather-like touches of his tongue. Each touch set her more and more on fire, filled her with a great and yearning need for him to make their bodies one, just as their souls had been one for so many months.

But he stayed away, refrained from taking her that last final irrevocable step, until Emma reached down and caressed him, and by her own act led him inside her, covering his face and neck with kisses. With a great shuddering sigh he thrust into her, and she let out a moan of pure joy, wrapping his trunk with her legs and arms, holding him within her, their bodies at last one.

Slowly they began to move in perfect rhythm, allowing their ecstasy to build up gradually, savouring the perfect sweetness of every move until at last they could hold back no longer, and allowed their passion to rise to its inevitable and world-shattering climax, as Emma cried out in a frenzy of joy and fulfilment, and he buried his face between her breasts. Exhausted both mentally and physically, they lay, gathering their breath back, locked in one another's arms, murmuring their love until they slept.

# CHAPTER TWELVE

SPRING came late to Glasgow. Emma got out of her tiny bed in the attic of a tall tenement, and shivered as she reached for her dressing-gown. Outside the April streets were drab and grey, the sky was grey and all the houses were grey. An alien breeze sent scraps of newspaper and empty crisp bags scudding along the gutters. She lit her gas ring and made herself a cup of tea.

After breakfast of an orange and another cup of tea, she went out of her room to the battered communal telephone on the wall in the corridor, and phoned the nursing agency. 'Sister Sandiford here. Anything for me today?'

'Nothing yet, Sister Sandiford. You'll be at home if we need you?'

'I have to go out for a while.' She had to buy milk and bread. 'I'll phone in an hour or so.'

'That will be fine, Sister.'

The disembodied Glasgow voice sounded friendly. Maybe Emma could get to like being here. It was her own fault that she had not contacted Mac, but she still felt fragile about talking to anyone from Forrestall. She had sought this exile voluntarily, and as soon as she felt her emotions were under control she would apply to one of the big hospitals, where she knew she was well qualified to get a permanent job.

Next door to the dim little grocer's shop where she bought her loaf, a carton of milk and a little meat bridie for her lunch, there was an equally dim little café with a delicious smell of bacon, eggs and sausages drifting from the door. It was tempting, and she had nothing to do for an hour. Emma went in, and ordered a cooked breakfast. The other clients looked like shipyard shift workers, office cleaners, and yes, maybe one or two nurses just off nights.

Someone had left a newspaper on the table, and while she waited for her meal she opened it and glanced at the news. 'There you are, hen.' The cheerful woman who brought her breakfast was as homely and honest as the food. 'Nothing like a decent breakfast to start anyone's day.'

Emma thanked her, and folded the newspaper to lay on the table. It was open at the 'Personal' column, and under 'Deaths' a name she knew well caught her eye. She forgot the food, and seized the newspaper again, reading avidly. 'Elizabeth Ann Warwick, wife of Simon John and daughter of Pamela Quirke, at Forrestall, Lancs, after a short illness. Funeral private.'

She forgot breakfast. She made only two phone calls, one to the agency, resigning, and one to her mother, to say she was coming home.

Emma went straight to the Pendle Inn after settling her things back at home. 'I'd like to stay a few nights, Arthur, if that's OK?'

'Glad to have you, Emma. Ma will be right glad to have someone to cook for. She said you ought never to have gone to Scotland.'

'Yes, well, it seemed the right thing at the time,' smiled Emma, as she took her small bag up to the cosy room in the eaves. When she stood at the window, she could see through the wreaths of fresh green ivy the smiling face of the Pendle witch at close quarters. 'I'm on a level with you now, old lady. What can you do for me now? Please make things all right for Simon and me,' she murmured. It was a smooth green evening, with signs of spring all around, snowdrops growing profusely in the grey stone wall of the inn garden, and catkins shaking cheekily in the breeze. February's lambs were sturdier now, and the new corn was showing in the fields behind the inn. The witch smiled, and her ruddy cheeks glowed, but there was no sign of any magic.

Emma looked hard at the cutting which she had taken from the Scottish paper. There couldn't be any mistake. There was only one Simon Warwick at Forrestall with a wife called Elizabeth. Ma—Arthur's wife—whose first name nobody had ever known, came in with an extra pillow and a blanket. 'I know it's spring, but never cast a clout, love! I'll leave these here in case you need them.'

'Thanks, Ma. I won't stay long, but now that I'm back I'd like to be as close to—to my old friends as possible, until I can get myself a new job.'

'As long as you like, love. Your crowd still come in of a Saturday night, sometimes in the week too. Why don't you go and visit the nurses' flats? You're bound to see someone you know.'

'I'll do that.' But Emma didn't go to the nurses' flats. She put on her big designer sweater, jeans and a pair of woollen gloves, to walk in the gentle twilight along by the stone wall of the hospital to the back gates, where the Lodge stood, square and reliable, among the trees sporting their new leaves, and a hedge of blackthorn in sweet white blossom. It didn't look any different. Emma thought that perhaps it would have changed since losing one of its occupants. But there was no sadness about the Lodge, just its usual solid dependability, its changelessness, even to the old collie lying on the back step and wagging his tail gently as Emma neared him.

Could she just walk up to the door? There didn't seem to be any lights on. Maybe Simon had gone away after the funeral. She wouldn't blame him for that—he had been tied to Forrestall by a moral chain, and now that it was loosed he was free to go where he wished. Maybe he was still working? It was almost six o'clock. He always used to work till six. The nights were drawing out now, the evenings longer and sweeter as May hovered in the air.

She stood just inside the gates, invisible from the road, gazing at those blank windows, and recalling the night Simon had saved her, when Gareth Price had all but lost his life. A pair of wood pigeons were billing and cooing in a beech tree just above her, and further away the sweet mournful cry of an owl drifted through the trees. After a long time her feet grew cold, and she decided that Simon must be away. Why hadn't he got in touch? She couldn't see so well now, as twilight dimmed into night. She ought to have asked Ma or Arthur first, instead of being so disappointed. She walked back to the inn. But as she turned in to the entrance a green Jaguar sped by, and her heart beat faster. She turned to look—recognising the number-plate—but then wished she hadn't. In the passenger seat of the green Jaguar sat a very blonde woman.

She would have gone straight up to bed, but in the bar she saw Bill Kenyon, his fatherly face wreathed in smiles, and his foot up on the foot-rest at the bar. He was with another doctor whose name Emma didn't know, and they were talking about Simon. She crept in without being seen, and found that corner seat by the fire, where the weeping fig was bigger than ever, and provided her with a perfect shield.

'No, he never told a soul. I don't think he minds people knowing now. It had to come out that the poor lady was without a memory for years. Nobody realised that she had a chest infection until it had advanced into pneumonia. We were just too late with antibiotics. Thank God she never suffered. She just couldn't get up one morning when he went to wake her. He called me in, and we got her into the medical wing at once. She was already in a coma, and though she lingered for three days there was really no hope of her coming round.'

'The memory loss—did that have anything to do with the illness?'

'Surely. She wouldn't remember what pneumonia was, so she couldn't tell anyone. Simon said she never coughed, and he had no reason to check her heart and lungs.' Bill finished off his pint. 'I'm always sorry when a patient dies, but in this case I can't help but see it was a blessed release for both of them.'

And as Arthur filled up their glasses the two men went on to speak of hospital matters. Emma sat quietly, waiting for them to go before she crept up to bed. She remembered that Simon had ordered her to go out with as many boys as she wanted—he had told her not to waste her youth. Maybe he was taking his own advice. Maybe the blonde was the first of many, as Simon celebrated his freedom. But he could have let Emma know. . . It was cruel, finding out from a discarded newspaper.

Next day was so beautiful, the sun so warm and the fields so green, the sky the colour of Simon Warwick's eyes, and the birds singing their little hearts out, that Emma somehow could not be sad. She would wait until

Simon got home that evening, and boldly knock on his door. She had every reason to. She had come out of respect, as a friend, to offer condolences. Meanwhile, she would go for a long walk on the moors she loved, and forget the troubles and uncertainties that had plagued her since the first time she had faced Simon Warwick across the tennis court in the late days of last summer.

The walk did her good. It was good to feel the sun on her back, to smell the fresh grass and the may blossom in the hedgerows. She was sitting inside the inn in late afternoon, having tea and teacakes at one of the picnic tables Arthur always put out in good weather. She had hoped to see Simon right away, and it was frustrating to sit around and wait for him. Perhaps she ought to go into Personnel and let them know that she wanted to come back to Forrestall. She thought for a while. No, until she had seen Simon she knew there could be no arrangements made. That blonde might be his steady. After all, Emma had been away long enough for Simon to meet someone else. She looked up at the witch. The sign hung perfectly still against a clear blue sky, and the witch appeared not to meet Emma's eyes. You cheat! You brought me back for nothing, accused Emma silently, as she pushed away her second buttered teacake.

At exactly six, the time when Simon always used to go home, she set off once more to walk round the hospital walls towards the Lodge. This time her chin was up. This time she was determined to walk straight in and knock on the door. Her confidence had returned. Perhaps that blonde was just someone he was giving a lift to. Her step quickened, and she began to believe that he would be there, to imagine the look of surprise and happiness in his eyes. . .

She heard footsteps outside the Lodge door, and hesitated, then concealed herself behind the blackthorn hedge. It would be nice to see him without being seen, and then come out of the trees to surprise him. . . Then the footsteps came nearer, and she realised they were light, woman's footsteps, and not Simon's at all. In a blaze of elegant black dress and shimmering diamonds, Caroline Brett came up to the door and knocked.

Emma's heart beat painfully as the door opened and Simon, looking relaxed in a polo shirt and jeans, appeared. He smiled, and Emma's heart hurt even more at that familiar lean face, the twinkle in the blue eyes. 'Caroline, you're early! I'm not even changed. You look very beautiful tonight.'

'Well, I have to wear black out of respect.'

'It suits you. Come on in, and help yourself to a drink while I get changed.'

Emma didn't wait. Once the door had closed, she turned and hurried back to the inn. It was true—he was reacting to his freedom by playing the field! And he hadn't even tried to get in touch with her. She felt tears sting her eyes, and tried to blink them away as she walked. She looked up at the witch and almost stamped her foot in misery and frustration. You're such a fraud! she raged silently. Where's that special relationship, then? Why isn't he here, why doesn't he sense that I'm here? Because I imagined it all, that's why. I was so besotted that I was willing to believe there was something special between us. Well, now I know! Thank goodness I didn't go back to the hospital. I'll never work here again. I'll see my mother and then I'll go back to London and forget there ever was a Simon Warwick.

* * *

'Will you be wanting dinner, love?' Ma did all the cooking at the inn. 'I've just made a steak and kidney pie. Or there's a pheasant Arthur brought in this afternoon?'

'I'm not hungry, Ma,' said Emma. But the fragrance of that pie filled the little snug. 'Well, just a little piece, then.' She ate the home-cooked meal, a meal fit for a queen, without tasting it. It could have been sawdust. Afterwards she went and sat in the once special corner seat, and Arthur brought her a brandy and soda. 'Thanks, Arthur.'

'Well, you're looking a bit down in the mouth, Emma. This is on the house, with instructions to enjoy it.'

She smiled at him. The inn was just beginning to fill up with the evening crowd. 'I've always liked this place. I thought it was the witch that brought it that bit of magic—but I know now it's your good heart and Ma's good cooking.'

Arthur looked at her knowingly. 'And you've never once asked me if Mr Warwick still comes in for his usual pint,' he said with kindly eyes. 'I can't believe that you're not curious. You were that close, once. Like as though you knew what the other one was thinking.'

'You see more than you let on, you rogue.'

'He doesn't come in as often—like his life has broadened out, as it were. And not before time. But he comes in all right, when he's got a spare minute, like. I've noticed he never brings anyone else—always comes alone.'

'None of his other girls, you mean?' Emma tried to be practical. 'Don't pretend, Arthur. I know he's got girlfriends.'

Arthur looked back at the bar, where people needed serving. Then he turned back and said, 'There's girlfriends and there's girlfriends, Emma. Don't you forget that!'

'It doesn't bother me in the slightest,' she lied to his retreating back.

But as she sat there, as other customers came and went, her feelings grew so that she felt as though she couldn't contain them. Someone had put a tape on, and the words of a love song cut into her soul.

She stirred herself from her reverie. It was almost closing time, and Arthur was collecting glasses. She thought it was Arthur standing at the table, but when she looked up she looked into Simon's eyes. 'I came as soon as I could,' he said simply.

'How did you know——?' But she didn't complete the question. She knew how he knew. The same way that she had come to him that first night. She looked out of the window. The witch was grinning. She looked back at Simon. 'Would you like to sit down?' He was in a dinner-jacket and black tie. Of course, he had invited Caroline in while he got changed. Some special function, then. There would be no doubt that they made a handsome couple, Simon and Caroline. . .

Arthur called across the room, 'I've locked up, Emma. Put the light out when you come up.' He put the lights out over the bar, and he and Ma went up to bed. The fire had gone out, but the room was full of a strange warmth, and the small table lamp cast shadows behind the weeping fig.

Simon sat opposite to her and held out his hands. She allowed him to take hers and hold them tightly. She wanted to feel happy, but happiness wouldn't come. She said formally, 'I haven't offered my condolences.'

'Thank you.' He waited, but she had mental pictures of that blonde girl, and of Caroline Brett in that revealing gown, and couldn't think of anything to say. He said, 'I thought you'd be glad to see me.'

She nodded, in spite of herself. 'I'm glad to see you looking so—well.'

'But? Why the hesitation?'

'Why didn't you let me know yourself?'

'Why, darling girl? Because you'd disappeared from the face of the earth, as far as I could find out. Your mother had no address. She said you just phoned her from time to time and said you were all right. I telephoned every hospital in Glasgow, because I thought that was where you were going. Nobody had ever heard of you! What were you doing, Sandy? Where were you? I was out of my head for days, when nobody knew where you were.'

She realised that he hadn't contacted her because he hadn't known where she was, because she had given no one her address or phone number. 'I'm sorry—I didn't think—I was working for an agency.'

'Why?'

'Well—for a couple of months I thought I might be pregnant, so it would be silly to start a permanent job.'

His face worked and he held her hands even tighter. 'Oh, no! Oh, what have I done? Sandy, my own darling, you should have come straight back to me. We might have had our own baby.'

'Well, it turned out not to be pregnancy. I—just—just missed a couple of months because——'

'I know, darling, I know. Your emotions were in a mess. So were mine. What a ghastly time you must have gone through. But you should have come to me. Who else could you go to? You needed someone. . .'

'It's all right now. I'm sorry. I forgot you didn't have

my phone number. And there I was, blaming you for not getting in touch.'

'So why did you come back now, love?'

'It's funny. It was quite by accident that I picked up a newspaper in a café and saw the announcement.'

He smiled broadly. 'Not quite by accident, my Sandy. I'm glad it worked. I put that notice into all the Scottish papers for two weeks. They must have thought I was daft, but I couldn't think how else to find you.'

She began to feel slightly better. 'So you did want to find me Simon?'

'Doesn't it sound like it.'

'A bit.'

'A bit! Sandy, if you weren't back by the time I take my holidays in May, I was going to spend those holidays looking for you. I suppose I would have got round to checking the agencies then.'

'It really sounds as though you meant it.' She looked at him longingly. 'I want to believe it. But, Simon, I've been here two days. On the first day there was a beautiful blonde in your car. Tonight there was Caroline Brett looking like something from Hollywood, and you looking delighted to see her, and inviting her in. What was I to think?'

It was quite dark now, but the moon was full and its rays flooded in through the leaded windows and cast shadows on the stone walls of the inn. Simon stood up and moved round to sit next to her, and took her face gently between his hands. He kissed her lips very slowly, tasting them with his warm mouth and tongue, as he had that first day in the rain. 'My only sweetest love, the blonde in my car was my ugly mother-in-law, and I was taking her to catch her train back to the Costa del

Crime after she relented and came to thank me for what I'd done for Liz.'

'Oh.'

He smiled and kissed her again, for longer. 'And tonight there was a fund-raising dinner in aid of Park Hall Wing, and I owe them an awful lot for all the help they've given me over the years.'

'You didn't have to go with Caroline.'

'You sound jealous, Sandy. Don't ever be jealous, darling girl. Remember there's a very big difference between friends and lovers.' His voice was deep and husky. 'And you know which you are.'

'I think I do. I know I do.'

He smiled, and his face was relaxed and happy, almost like that day when they had walked around Manchester like teenagers, and ate cheeseburgers and had their photographs taken. As though reading her mind he opened his wallet and brought out the photograph and laid it on the table. Two happy people. . . 'I think I got your "message" about nine or nine-thirty. I was chatting to Bill Kenyon when something made me stop and your face came into my head. I came away as soon as it was polite. Alone. Caroline's getting a lift from Bill and his wife.'

Emma looked at his dear familiar face in the moonlight and put both arms round his neck. 'I never want to let you go again,' she murmured into his dinner-jacket.

'Don't worry, nobody's going anywhere. I guess we'll have to wait six months to be married, but I'm not letting my wise woman out of my sight in case you disappear again. You did say you would marry me?'

'I said you know the answer to that.'

'Say it, darling. Say it now. Say what I wished I was free to hear right from the beginning.'

She said it. 'I love you with all my soul, Simon, and the only thing I want in the world is to be your wife and to care for you for the rest of my life.'

He held her very tightly, and she felt the wetness of tears on his cheek. She whispered, 'It's been hell for you for too long, Simon darling. From now on I'll make it the complete opposite—I swear it.'

After a while he managed to say, 'Didn't Arthur tell you to put the lights off?'

'Oh, yes.' They both smiled at the thoughtfulness of the old landlord. Emma would have disentangled herself from her Simon, but he wouldn't let her go. 'All right, we'll do it together.' And they put off the lights in the little snug, leaving the moonlight to dapple the walls and the tiled floor, while he carried her upstairs to bed.

This time he was too impatient to be slow, and undressed her with quick trembling hands. 'You're mine, my love. Say you're mine, and show me.' Already aroused, they came together with a new delight and joy, tears mingling with laughter and passion as at last they were able to give vent to the mightiness of their emotions and the heights of their love.

In the early hours of the morning, impatient desire at last giving way to a languorous lethargy, Simon stroked her body with his fingers as he lay back on the pillows, his darling's head lying on his breast. He whispered, 'I'm sorry I shouted at you, Sandy.'

'Shouted? When did you shout at me?'

'That day when you took my parking space.'

Emma giggled, and tried to stifle her giggles in the bedsheet. 'Believe it or not, that's when I knew that in some strange way you were always going to be important to me.'

He said, pretending to be serious, 'I think now is the time for me to admit that you can take my parking space any time you wish.'

She rolled over on top of him. 'Thanks for that. And what else can I have, while you're in this generous mood?' She smoothed back his hair from his hot forehead and kissed it.

He reached up and cupped her face in his hands. 'My life. All of my life. Oh, Sandy, Sandy, at last I have a real life—and it's yours. There can't be anyone in this world as fortunate as I am tonight.'

'As fortunate as you? What about me?'

'That's the best of all. No more me and you. From now on, there'll only be us.'

Emma looked out of the window into the smiling face of the Pendle witch. 'There always was, darling. We just took a little while to believe it, that's all. It seemed a little bit far-fetched at first, but it wasn't. It was just true.'

'I know. Kiss me, my wise woman. Kiss me until I beg for mercy, Sandy. There's a lot of wasted time to make up.'

She kissed him. After a long time she whispered, 'I'm glad we came here. That old witch has been waiting a long time for this. But you could always tell that she meant to get her own way, couldn't you? Even when we fought her, she knew what was meant to be, and she never gave up.'

Simon rolled over, newly aroused and meeting her ardour with his. 'You and your fairy-stories. . .'